# What Was Left
A collection of short stories and flash fictions

Edited by Amanda Saint and Jane Elmor

A Retreat West Books publication

Dedicated to all lovers of short, and very short, stories

# Contents

# Foreword

## Amanda Saint and Jane Elmor

Putting together this first collection of stories from the inaugural RW Short Story Prize and RW Flash Fiction Prize has been a real pleasure. We are honoured that the writers of all the stories included here submitted their work to us for the 2016 Prizes and have enabled the creation of this anthology, which is a wonderful example of the many different approaches and styles being used in short form fiction today.

Particular congratulations go to the winners in each category and our thanks to the judges, Vanessa Gebbie for the short stories and David Gaffney for the flash fictions.

The title of the anthology, *What Was Left*, comes from a shortlisted story from Joanna Campbell and was chosen as we feel it hints at what is left unsaid and what sits around and beneath the stories that are told here.

Judith Wilson was the overall winner of the Short Story Prize with her haunting tale of loss, *On Crosby Beach*. Vanessa said: 'I found myself coming back to this atmospheric piece time and time again, seeing something different in it each time I re-read. It is a story about loss on several levels, about loss of innocence, about living with guilt which will not leave, and about an attempt at resolution and atonement.'

In contrast, Ian Tucker's second place story, *Honeysuckle Happiness Hospice*, is a comedy about the lengths people will go to for money. Vanessa said: 'This one is clever, it is pacy, laugh out loud funny, and written entirely in emails, documents and texts … This one really keeps you hanging on waiting for the next message!'

Third place went to Veronica Bright's poignant story told in a list, *Ten Things I Can Tell You About Abraham Lincoln*. Vanessa said: 'A neat very short piece, proving you don't need to use all the words available to tell a good story. Certainly, this is an example of making every word earn its place, and by the end, I felt I knew these characters and their lives better than those in some novels!'

Vanessa also gave an honorary mention to Alec Hutson's, *Under The Banyan Tree*, saying: 'I thought the characters were well drawn, and that the scenes had been carefully and successfully crafted to elicit maximum emotion from the reader. It certainly punches above its weight.'

For the Flash Fiction Prize, David Gaffney chose the quietly powerful and moving, *At The Hospital*, by Jude Higgins as the winner, saying: 'An intimate and moving encounter between a young girl and her dying grandparent, and the way it focuses on the minutiae of the scene – the grape she is peeling for her granddad, the colour of his skin, the bird outside the window opening and closing its beak – create an emotionally powerful vignette.'

In second place, *Keep Calm and Carry On*, by Emily Richards is another comedy, this time shining a light on how interactions in society today can seem to be purely driven by clichés. David said: ' I like the accumulation of detail and pop culture references and the way different voices appear to be batting about in the character's head like he is exploding with other people's points of view and can't find his own.'

The third prize for flash fiction went to Mandy Huggins for her breathless and joyful story with a melancholy undertone about friendship and regrets, *Giddy With It*. David said: 'Lots of great texture about clothes and music and brands of the time and a really nice story tucked underneath all of this about a band made up of two best friends that sort of existed and didn't exist, all at the same time, like Schrodinger's cat.'

While these are the stories chosen by the judges, every story here in this collection is, we believe, a fine one. We hope you agree.

# What Was Left

Joanna Campbell

Hilary tucked her baby's blanket under its chin. She wondered if the thick woollen folds were pressing on its windpipe. Not that she could imagine the gristly tube, or whatever a windpipe looked like, beneath the fat folds of its neck. She wondered; but she left it there, just as she also left the scalloped edge of the bonnet to flop over its eyes. It cried when it couldn't see.

Rain pelted on the pram. Hilary's old mackintosh smelt of the old biscuit crumbs caught in the pocket seams and of steaming with friends by the classroom boiler, watching the corridor in case Joe sauntered by. The sleeves ended at her elbows, but an eighteen-year-old widow's money didn't stretch to new coats. Every spare coin clinked into a rinsed-out jam-jar with Rent scratched on the lid.

Joe's bicycle had known every dip in the road to the factory where he made coal-scuttles. But six months ago, his front wheel stopped short on a sudden stone.

Motherhood was the same; a boulder on a road once clear. Joe's stone sent him into the path of the dawn quarry bus. Just before he left the house, he had seen his baby's first primitive smile.

Hilary might as well have been the one flung over the handlebars and under the screaming tyres. She and Joe were two book-ends, one indispensable to the other, both essentially the same. Now she was alone, she missed him. But most of all, she missed herself.

Joe was a man for all people, tipping out cigarettes for his friends, slapping them on the back. Friday nights at the Cock and Bull, he was first at the bar and last to leave. First to drum up a sing-song. Last to end it with his dark-brown rendering of Day Is Done. He even impersonated the bugle.

As the moon slithered through the elms, he sang his way home. High spirits, it was. Joe drank orange-squash. He had promised Hilary, no hard stuff. Her own Da had pickled in whisky like a walnut in vinegar, his brain the crinkled husk, his liver the poisoned kernel. At forty he took his short-cut home through the churchyard and withered away on a freshly dug hummock, a dead spit for a bundle of jumble. Hilary's Ma allowed no sherry at the wake.

Joe died a more graceful death, according to the landlady of the Cock and Bull, who witnessed the elegant cartwheel over his handlebars while she was scrubbing her step and sent Hilary a platter of funeral sandwiches garnished with the ash that fell from her cigarette.

When the tea-pot emptied and the bridge rolls wilted, most people left Hilary's house, although a straggle of pub regulars loitered, hopeful something fiery might yet be uncorked. Hilary would rather have sat in the pitch-black cradling Joe's old jersey, the smell of him knitted into it.

The wake disbanded, the lights of the Cock and Bull flickering on as Hilary's house darkened. In the garden, the string of damp, white towelling squares swayed like bunting for a ghost's party.

Days clogged up against nights. Weeks welded together in an endless block. No bright moments seared holes in the gloom. No dreams mattered. The baby's wails kept wrenching Hilary out of her memories.

Sometimes it smiled its foolish smile and always drank like a whale. Dorothy brought lean ham to put meat on Hilary's bones, and teething-rings made of ham-bone for the baby's tender gums. Everything was white and pink and pulsing with life, except Hilary's heart, which folded over, crinkling like a deflated balloon.

Her schoolgirl mackintosh reeked of old happiness. Watching Joe arrive at school on his bicycle. Kissing under the birch that hung over the iron gates. Wishing the bell would never ring.

Once she had squeezed into the wedding-gown Ma threw together from a houseful of net curtains, a gown that failed to conceal the fast-inflating beach-ball of Joe's baby, folk set aside their disapproval. Women no longer sniffed, noses aloft. They tore up their tired sheets, hemming them into crib-size squares. They found spare wool for bonnets, including the one making the baby itchy and cross now as Hilary pushed the pram up the hill to Woolworth's.

Other babies blew bubbles and grinned, but Hilary's frowned all the way. She passed Mrs Tremlett and her gabbling little Bobby in his lime cardigan. And there was Melanie Morris in her polka-dot trenchcoat, chattering to her Ingrid who could already sit up and point at birds.

People smiled at Hilary now six months — the allotted time for grief — had passed. They no longer whispered in her presence as if they were in the chapel of rest. She had, they assumed, inched her way up the bitter hump of sorrow that cast such a cold shadow at first. By now she should have clambered to its summit and begun the tricky, yet hopeful, descent to smoother ground where sunlight fingered its way into every corner. Clothing of a lighter colour would soon be tolerated and Hilary could emerge from her half-year trek through the dark. Such was the etiquette of mourning.

But Hilary had curled into a corner of herself before Joe died, her widow's grief a smokescreen for the terror which reared as soon as the child slithered from her body.

Joe had hushed its cries, rocked it until the navy-blue eyes stopped staring. Hilary was emptied of herself as if, when her waters ruptured, her soul had also come away.

Woolworth's was between Fleet's shoe-repairs and Philip-the-fish. When Hilary and Joe used to line up for haddock on Saturdays, Joe liked to keep the queue in stitches.

'What kind of fish makes you hear better, Mrs Tremlett? I'll tell you, shall I? A herring-aid! And why is a sword-fish's nose eleven inches long, d'you think, Mrs Morris? Because if it were twelve inches, it'd be a foot!'

Joe reckoned Philip always slapped the fish with the keenest eye into their basket.

'No need to weigh it, Phil. Got its own scales!' he would say, turning round to an ocean of smiles.

Sometimes Philip would tip out a half-pint of prawns and wrap them at half-price. Hilary could hear them now, rasping onto the white paper while Philip gave her a gentle wink. Joe shelled the prawns in the sink and when he rinsed them, it washed the salty scent of the sea into their kitchen. He doused them with malt vinegar to cut through the sweetness and Hilary sat on his lap while he posted them into her mouth.

Hilary guessed people had long since tired of Joe's stubborn good cheer. They prayed to God he would just smile and nod in passing, just as they tried to do. His jokes often floundered, but he never knew when to stop.

Regulars at the Cock and Bull used his good nature to cadge a cigarette, a drink, a song for the late evening when their own conversations flagged. Her own Da had called Joe a pushover. Joe called himself the luckiest bloke in the world. The sun rose and set with his young wife and baby. He would never have imagined anyone rolling a stone in his path, just out of mischief, to quell his shrill dawn whistling. But Hilary sometimes wondered, threading her thoughts through a needle, but not stitching them together.

The fish didn't always have such a keen eye and the prawns were half-drowned in a puddle of melted ice from the previous day. But what mattered was that Joe warmed himself in the glow of imagined affection and Hilary missed his optimism. She missed that most of all.

She parked the pram on the slope outside Woolworth's, pressing her foot on the brake until the wheels locked. She didn't fret about it rolling away. Fretting unpicked a stray loop of thought that it mightn't matter really if the brakes failed.

The baby was screaming, arching, flailing, its face purple and creased like a fallen plum on the road. It wrinkled its nose at the smell of haddock and hake, snubbing the spot where it was supposed to lie in peace while its mother grazed in the pastures of plastic measuring jugs and trays of toffee and assorted coat-hangers.

People glanced, ignoring the red mop-and-bucket sets on display in the store-window. Tutting and muttering, they peered instead at the mound of child thrashing about under the pram-covers.

Hilary stroked the solid coachwork and the water-repellent hood that allowed raindrops to stand proud for hours, reflecting rainbows that evaporated in the sun. If only she could crawl inside the bottle-green cave, she would relish the batter of rain on her roof while some other pair of hands guided her up and down the hill.

The carriage rocked and the child screeched, but Hilary picked up her shopping basket and carried it into the store. In between taking in shoes for new soles and lining up for Dover soles, passers-by would wave and coo, bestowing their infinite patience on the babies left to wail outside Woolworth's.

Perhaps, Hilary thought, someone lonely, maybe someone a little touched in the head, would dig their hands into the blankets, pluck out the child like a damp shrimp from its papery skin and take it away.

The doors swung open. The Woolworth womb closed around Hilary. Steam rising from the penny buns smelt of a time so magical it set her free again. She ran her hand over zip-fasteners and cards of pink elastic, around the edges of price labels. At the Pick and Mix, bluebirds flew on toffee wrappers and Gainsborough ladies smiled from caramels.

As she reached the bleach-scented aisle of cleaning products, the strip-lights buzzed and flickered. Customers gibbered about the storm gathering pace.

'It's turning electric,' someone said to a chorus of gasps.

Confectionary scoops hovered in mid-air. Paper bags stopped rustling. The lights failed. After a brief silence, there was a tentative murmuring.

But without warning a spear of lightning pierced the store with frightening white light. Women screamed and ran out, dropping baskets, abandoning friends. Like iron filings to a magnet, hands seized hold of pram handles and reassuring voices cooed.

Hilary stayed by the Jeyes Fluid.

'Bring the babes inside, ladies,' the manager called, drawing himself up to his full five feet four, the keeper of his castle. 'Try not to drip on the merchandise, my dears. Come on, come back inside. Normal service will be resumed.'

Consulting his sales target on a sheet of paper clipped to a piece of shirt cardboard, he paced the sales floor, nodding like a rooster at the rows of little bald heads and round-eyed toddlers unshackled from their pram-seats.

'Cloaks please, Adrienne,' he said.

A round-shouldered girl trundled out a clothes-rail clanking with wire-hangers. The ladies festooned it with their rain-soaked coats. Adrienne nibbled her left thumb knuckle while her right hand roamed inside the damp pockets.

'Bring out that Christmas tin of shortbread-fingers, Adrienne, and pass it round,' the manager said.

Although the fingers were stale now it was April, they helped the crowd turn the fright into an impromptu party.

'It'll pass, the storm,' the manager said. 'Never fear. Those prams'll take the downpour all right. Got your covers drawn up tight? The sun'll drip-dry that good canvas in no time. Comes with a guarantee if you bought them here, you know.'

Prams were not admitted to the store once bought and wheeled from the premises. No rubbery tracks would soil his flooring. No sodden hoods would brush against his Bri-nylons.

'I allowed a double-carriage in once and never got all the marks off my spring range of quilted housecoats,' he said.

Babies were set down to play pat-a-cake and picked up to be soothed. Children crumbled shortbread into the special-offer saucepans. Conversations moved from Tupperware to Torquay. The sun shone for the women and children long before it reappeared in the sky.

The manager rescued the display mops from two small boys jousting.

'Adrienne, we need eyes everywhere. Anything could be lifted in this dim light,' he muttered.

Adrienne continued clearing grime out of her fingernails with the point of a pencil.

Unnoticed, Hilary walked through the centre aisle to the rhythm of the flashes and overhead crashes, all the way to the other set of doors at the back. She left the store, her face defying the torrent, and pelted down the hill towards home.

With no pram to drag up the cobbled lane and wrestle through her front door, she was unburdened. She could go inside all by herself.

'I'm home!' she cried. 'Joe, I'm back!'

She opened a tin of beef broth, set the pan on the gas and lit the fire, all without having to put her hands over her ears, without having to unfasten her clothes in a rush and feel the face like a wet rose on her breast.

She sat by the hearth, cradling the soup-bowl in her hands long after the heat had left it. The fire died down. Tiny, determined flames devoured the embers. The more they consumed, the smaller they became. Not like the baby, equally gluttonous, but persistently bursting out of its garments like fried sausage from its skin.

Hilary's chest tightened at the thought and a spot of milk leaked. She shivered. It was the milk of guilt.

The flames squealed before shrivelling away. The coal-scuttle was empty and now spring was coming, the bunker contained a heap of black dust. It was time to pull the screen across the hearth.

'Joe, come and sit by this last fire with me,' she called. 'It's all quiet. The baby's asleep.'

More milk oozed.

'We don't have long, Joe. Quick before it dies.'

When only her own voice answered, she fell silent. Within the final flame, Da appeared, a half-remembered face, a younger version of the broken man found on the moss. The Da in the fire once read his daughter fables, her face reflected in his glasses.

The embers crumbled. As Hilary turned away from what was left, reaching for the screen, a new fire spluttered into life. One jubilant flame lit the room, roared for a minute and left without dying, as if it had vanished here to burn somewhere else. For sixty defiant seconds, it had burned for Hilary.

People passed her window in the freshening air. No one hurried now. Umbrellas dripped by their sides. Transparent rain-bonnets hung like dead jellyfish in their hands.

Hilary was still sitting in her mackintosh when she heard the rattle of pram-wheels over the cobbles.

Dorothy pushed open the door.

'Ah, Hilary. You must be frantic, dear. I can see you're about to rush back now the storm's settled. But no need. I've got Baby here. None the worse for wear. I imagine you were frightened by that awful thunderclap and made a mad dash for it. Quite understandable. I have an aunt who needs smelling-salts at the first rumble.'

Hilary went to the door. Unflinching raindrops were sitting on the pram's hood. They would dissolve in the sun and leave no trace, as if they were never there.

'My dear,' Dorothy said, 'I know everyone expects you to feel brighter now, but grief takes its own time. I see you're still in your black.'

'Yes,' Hilary said, 'I'm still in it.'

They stood on the step while the baby beat its fists on the pram cover.

'It's cold. Why don't you put a warm cardigan on,' Dorothy said, peeling off Hilary's mackintosh.

'Joe gave me a lovely green one for my last birthday.'

'Then you should consider wearing it, dear. Only you know when the time feels right, but I'm sure Josie will love seeing you in a cheerful colour.'

'And Joe had this bright red jumper, but it's far too big for me.'

'Then unravel it, dear. And reknit it tighter.'

'You have to take it apart from where it ends, don't you?' Hilary asked. 'From where you bound off?'

'Oh yes. If you start from the other direction, you'll be working against yourself, dear. And when you wash the yarn afterwards, leave it soaking wet to drip. You need the weight of the water to straighten it out. It'll look pitiful, but that's all part of the process.'

Dorothy rattled her bunch of keys to amuse Josie and said what a great soprano for the church choir she would be one day.

'I remember you being born, dear,' she said to Hilary. 'What a

20

blessing you were for your mother through the years.'

Josie stopped wriggling to listen, agape like a startled goldfish.

'Can you see what I see?' Dorothy asked.

Hilary nodded. There, in doll-like miniature, was Joe's face.

'Here,' Hilary said. 'Come to Mother, Josie.'

Josie's fingers clamped like starfishes to her mother's cheeks, the way Joe used to cup them in his hands, pushing up the corners of her mouth to make her smile.

She had smelt whisky in the mist of his breath. Morning and night. People whispered that when he was cycling to work that last morning, young Joe was still in his cups from the night before. They said he had never kept his promise to his poor young wife.

But the future wasn't about what people said, what story they made of all that had gone. It was about what was left.

'The storm is passing on, dear,' Dorothy said. 'I'm going back up the hill to collect my galoshes and a nice trout. It'll be normal service at Woolworth's by now. Shall I fetch you anything?'

The worn-out clouds were disbanding and the sun appeared, a pale lemon balloon. Philip-the-fish might sell her a small fillet and, now time had passed, he might start winking at her again. She could smile back, to show…to show him… She left the thought unstitched for now and laid Josie in her pram. She took off the cover, shook it dry and, clipping it back on, said, 'No thank you, Dorothy. We'll walk with you back up the hill.'

# The Cottage on the Hill

## Heather Walker

I hated living in the countryside, all those trees mocking, their whispered words breeze-blown to my doorway. When the wind raged, which it often did on this hill, their anger hurtled down chimneys and through cracks of the ill-fitting doors and windows. Despite this, and the constant feeling that I was never alone, I did not think things could get worse. How wrong I was.

We'd moved here because of Morgan's job. He'd grown up in the countryside and missed it when he'd come to London to work. He couldn't bear the noise, the commute on jam-packed tube and bus. Morgan longed to return to the countryside of his childhood.

As for me, I loved London, and the Northern and Central Lines became a second home to me as I travelled to Grey's Inn Court where I worked as a secretary for a Barrister's chambers overlooking the green square, so peaceful in such a harried city. Yet, I adored the harriedness of it, the men in dark suits, the young in ripped jeans, the tourists with their cameras.

When Morgan announced that he had put in for a transfer to a cell branch in York the air was blue with my rantings. He said it would be good for us. A great place to bring up children, he told me. I wasn't ready yet for the house with roses round the door, home baking and tiny clones of ourselves running riot in the herb garden. I tried to tell Morgan that. He laughed.

One weekend we drove to York. I felt Morgan unwind the further we drove. At the same time I became tense as hedges closed in on us and crows circled and cawed. They seemed to echo my thoughts. This was not the place for me.

We saw three houses while we were there. One was in the city. It was a new build and Morgan hated it. The second one was just out of the city, a cottage. Morgan liked this but it needed so much work that we had neither the time nor the money to do it. The third was a cottage in the countryside. Morgan fell for it straightaway. Set on a hill it looked down towards the city. Morgan spouted on about the air, the space, the quaintness of it. He was hooked. I pointed out that this place, a three bedroom dilapidated thatched cottage, needed more spending on it than the cottage in the city. It was like Morgan chose not to hear my protests as we took in the peeling paint, the damp patch in the bathroom, the musty smell in the kitchen and the lack of modern heating.

I tried to reason with Morgan as we walked around the neglected garden. The sun was shining. It was high summer and the wild flowers were a spread of riotous colour. Morgan was ecstatic, but I was thinking of cold winters, no proper heating, the isolation and the trees bending in the wind, tapping against the windows. I told Morgan my fears. He took my hands. I could feel the energy coursing through him. He smiled.

'I don't feel safe here,' I told him.

'Nonsense,' he said rubbing my hands which were cold even in the heat of the day. 'This is the safest place on earth. Look at that.' He let go of one hand and spread his fingers to the green fields and the mocking trees. 'Who could not want to live here with these views?'

Me, I thought. This place does not like me. I felt it breathing around me as I'd walked through the rooms. The wooden floor objected to my footsteps. The cottage knew my feelings about it and it was letting me know those feelings were reciprocated.

Over dinner that night Morgan and I argued over the move. I was still angry that he had sought a transfer without consulting me first and now I was trying to convince him that if we had to make the move we should at least buy a house in the city - one we didn't have to spend a fortune on to make liveable. I threatened to let him go alone and his face crumpled. Suddenly he was all sorrow and apologies. He hadn't realised how this would impact on me, he said.

That night as we held each other we came to a compromise. We would give it a year. If then I still hated it we would move either into the city or back to London. Morgan could seek another transfer, if necessary. He promised me that and reluctantly I agreed. He really wanted this move and I should at least give it a go.

We put in an offer on the cottage on the hill and it was accepted. Everything moved fast. Far too fast for me. I resigned from the job I so loved, Morgan's company paid for the move and by the end of November we took all our possessions to the cottage on the hill.

I hated the silence. Morgan loved it. I heard the house whispering, Morgan heard the house settling for the night. He was used to this, he told me; these old places were like living organisms. I could believe that. It unnerved me and I slept badly. The wind brushed branches on the windows, and angry words raged down the chimneys telling me I was not wanted here. Morgan just laughed at my concerns. Said I had an over imaginative mind.

Christmas came. The fire burned brightly in the lounge. The tree helped cheer the room with its strings of tiny bright bulbs. I relaxed a little. I cooked a small turkey and we exchanged presents of warm jumpers and socks and vowed to look into getting some decent heating in the next year. We were, it seemed, making plans to stay.

New Year's Eve we were invited to a party by Morgan's work colleagues. It was the most fun I'd had since moving here. I hadn't yet found a job of my own. It wasn't that I was keen to spend all my time in the house. No, in fact I escaped each day and wandered the streets of York, took walks along the river and huddled in coffee shops to keep warm.

I was merry as we drove back home, relaxed. Rain was lashing the windscreen. Trees dipped and swayed in the wind. Morgan drove carefully in case any trees had been blown onto the road. We arrived safely to find our front door banging to and fro in the wind. We'd left the porch light on but now it had gone out. The house stared back eerily, the windows like gaping black mouths in the moonless night. Morgan never hesitated. He just walked in and put on the lounge light.

As I approached the door I noticed the porch light cover had broken and the bulb had shattered. I expected to see a broken lock on the door, but no.

'Well, we haven't been burgled,' Morgan said brightly, coming back and meeting me at the door. 'Come on Vanessa, it's just the wind. Come in and close the door. You're letting the cold in.'

I took a step closer and my foot caught something. I looked down at a piece of coal. I bent to pick it up. It was warm. My eyes scanned the darkness looking for something. Morgan came to see what was keeping me and dragged me in. 'For goodness sake, we'll never get the house warm if you stand out there all night.' I held out the piece of coal to Morgan without a word. 'What's that?' I handed it to him. 'It's warm.'

'Yes,' I said. 'It's the only warm thing in this house.' I felt too sober for my own good. I shivered. 'I'm going to bed.'

All night I shivered, the trees throwing down their mocking words at me, their limbs tapping at the window for my attention. Morgan had tried to convince me that the coal was a gift from one of the villagers – a New Year tradition, first footing, and of course we weren't in. Maybe he was right. Perhaps I was making too much of it. Now Morgan snored alongside me without a care.

I found a job in York, working for a Solicitor who seemed reluctant to bring his practice into the modern age. The building had no heating except electric fires and his filing system was the most chaotic I had ever had the misfortune to work with. I tried my best to organise him. Mr Green seemed reluctant to let me therefore he always overran his appointments, lost files, forgot clients and even forgot my name. His clients, though, forgave him all that because he was a sweet man, rather eccentric but pleasant and polite. Strangely he always came through for his clients in the end.

I became fond of Mr Green. He was a fatherly figure and work was a great solace from living in that cottage on the hill where the trees continued to whisper and odd things went missing (misplaced Morgan said) and where, even as the days lengthened and the sun flooded the countryside, the cottage remained cold and unwelcoming. Morgan never seemed to notice. Perhaps he was right about my imagination after all.

In the late spring Morgan decided to tackle the garden. It was dreadfully overgrown but each weekend he would be out there cutting, pruning, digging until we had a patch to plant and a space to sit, and to hang out the washing. He also got someone in to fix the damp patch in the bathroom, and we decorated the bedroom in yellow and white to lift the gloom I always felt there.

By summer Morgan was making great headway with the garden. We let some of the wild flowers stay and brought the rest under control. The only part remaining uncultivated was the very bottom of the garden in which an oak tree stood. When Morgan began to tackle it he found a low fence running across partitioning it from the rest of the garden. He pulled this up and used a scythe to cut the overgrowth. While doing this the scythe hit something hard. I was bringing a glass of lemonade to him as Morgan had been outside all morning without much of a break.

'Dinner's nearly ready,' I said.

Morgan looked up. 'Hit a flaming rock or something,' he complained. He crouched down and pulled away the grass. 'It will have to come up.'

I bent down to look. The top of the stone was rounded. I touched the surface. It was cold and rough. 'There's some sort of writing or pattern on here,' I said.

Morgan took a closer look. 'No, it's just wear and tear.' He stood up and laid the scythe aside and picked up the spade.

'Maybe we should just leave it.'

'It's in the way.' Morgan shoved the spade down deep into the soil. A flock of crows flew up from the field beyond the garden making me jump. Their calls made me nervous.

'Leave it, Morgan.'

'Don't be so dramatic. I'll have it out in no time.'

I walked away back into the house and sat at the kitchen table watching Morgan digging down and down. He came in for dinner and went straight back out. He'd complained that it was a 'bit of bugger' but insisted he would have it out soon now.

He didn't. Morgan worked out there all afternoon. When he came in he was sweaty and exhausted. 'It's in so deep, Vanessa. But I have dug a trench around it now. Tomorrow it will be out.'

In the morning while I was making tea I noticed the crows had landed in that patch of ground where the stone was. They had formed a circle around it. I walked out into the garden. When I reached the stone the crows flew away with hearty caws and watched me from the oak tree. Leaning across the trench I bent down and touched the stone again. It was warm. It reminded me of the piece of coal. The sun hadn't reached this part of the garden yet and I wondered whether the stone could still be holding the heat from yesterday. The trench Morgan had dug was several feet deep. Why would someone bury it so far down into the ground? I brushed the stone, inserting my fingers into what I was convinced was some sort of inscription. I thought about the previous owners. The house had been empty for a couple of years when we bought it. The agent had said that the man had died and there was no family. How sad. This wasn't a place I would want to live in on my own.

As I walked back to the house the crows came down from the tree and settled around the stone again. Was this a sign? My imagination was working overtime again.

Morgan set to work in the garden after a leisurely breakfast and I set about changing the bed and running the washing machine. I sat at the table flicking through a magazine. I was aware of how cold the kitchen had become. Something touched me. I turned. There was no one there. I let out a breath. It formed a cold vapour in front of me. I shivered. I stood up and looked out of the window. I felt a jolt as if something had passed through me, stretching my guts. I began to shake. A white trail twisted upwards and escaped through the window. I opened my mouth to shout but nothing came out.

I searched for Morgan at the bottom of the garden but I couldn't see him. I began to panic and ran out of the back door and down to where he had been working. Morgan was lying in the grass. At first I thought he was asleep but the angle of his legs wasn't right. I bent down. 'Morgan?' He groaned. I called his name again running a hand across his forehead. He was burning up. How long had he been lying here?

Morgan opened his eyes. 'Oh, I feel awful.'

'What happened?'

'I had the stone almost out. It was wriggling like a wonky tooth and then I lost my grip and slipped backwards. My head hurts.'

I helped Morgan to sit up and he put a hand to the back of his head. 'Ow. There's going to be one big lump there.'

I got him back to the cottage and put a cold flannel against his head. After a while he took some painkillers and decided to lie down. While Morgan was sleeping I went to have a look at the stone. It was leaning slightly to one side. The sun was streaming down now and the stone was giving off enough heat to fry an egg on. I gave it a kick with my foot and the crows rose from the oak, circled around me, calling and flying in close. I shooed them away but they continued to call flying closer. I felt the downdraught as they passed.

With my hands over my head I ran back to the cottage, my heart thumping wildly. I slammed the door on them. From the kitchen window I noticed that the crows had settled around the stone again. What was this all about? It was as if the stone did not want to be removed. Morgan should have listened to me in the first place and left well alone.

Later, when Morgan woke, I told him my theory.

'I'd have expected that from some born and bred villager but not from you, a hardened Londoner.' He smiled.

'It's not a joke, Morgan. I feel it. There is something in this house.'

'Well, I can't feel anything. I love this cottage.'

'Maybe I just pick up on things,' I suggested.

'You've never liked this cottage. You've always been negative and now you're looking for excuses.'

I was angry with Morgan for dismissing my fears once again. I had tried. I had almost started to believe that he had been right and that I was just too superstitious.

Yet the events of today told me that there was a presence in this cottage.

It was another week before Morgan had a chance to tackle the stone again. He would not listen to me. He'd spent a whole weekend on it previously and he wasn't about to give up now, he said. It was coming out whether it liked it or not.

'I don't think it does like it,' I said.

'Oh, not this again,' Morgan said and marched off down to the bottom of the garden.

Morgan never got to pull out the stone because a few minutes after he left the cottage the heavens opened. The storm that had threatened since yesterday broke and Morgan made a run for it back to the house.

After the storm had faded the crows gathered and started up their frantic calls. We tried to ignore them. There were more than usual and others seemed to be flying in. The whole of the bottom of the garden was alive with the big black things. While I thought it was scary, Morgan was just annoyed. He went upstairs and came down a minute later with his air rifle.

'No,' I said, 'you mustn't shoot them.'

'I'm just going to scare them.' Morgan opened the back door and the gun cracked across the sky. The crows flew up in one big mass, circled and headed towards the cottage. They were heading for us in a squawking cloud. Quickly I pulled Morgan back into the kitchen and slammed the door. There was an awful battering noise against the door and I screamed. A crow hit the kitchen window with force. I watched its body slide down the glass leaving behind a trail of blood and translucent fluid. The noise continued along with the dreadful calls. Then silence.

After ten minutes Morgan opened the back door and a heap of dead crows fell in onto the flagstone floor. I couldn't take much more of this. I fled upstairs leaving Morgan to shovel up the dead bodies.

We were quiet around each other. I thought this time Morgan must see what I meant. There was something sinister about this cottage and the ground surrounding it. The stone at the bottom of the garden was now left untouched and I was pleased.

Autumn slunk in. Nothing much had changed. Morgan was still happy in his job and I was at least content in mine. The trees still whispered; things in the cottage still disappeared; there were still cold spots in places. By late October the trees seemed to be shouting. I suggested to Morgan that our year was almost up and I wanted to move away, at least into the city. He didn't shout me down, but he didn't agree either.

'Give it a little longer, Vanessa. I still think we can make a go of it here.'

Did he?

That night I couldn't sleep. So much was going through my mind. I went down to the kitchen for a glass of water. I felt the chill hit me as I walked in and then I saw him standing by the window. I always expected ghosts to be see-through white wispy things. He was wearing sort of leggings, boots, a green tunic held at the waist with a brown leather belt. His hair was long and straggly. I could not see his face as he had his back to me.

I said 'Hello'. What else do you say? My heart was thumping. I don't know what I expected. He did not reply. He did not turn. Instead he walked through the wall and into the garden. I caught my breath and walked to the window. I could see him in the moonlight heading down towards the bottom of the garden where the stone was. And then he vanished.

It took me a long while to stop staring, searching for the man. When I returned to bed I tried to tell Morgan what I had seen but he just turned over with a mumble. He'd not taken in any of my words. I nuzzled my cold body into him, feeding off his warmth until I fell asleep.

The next morning I went down to the bottom of the garden. It must have rained in the night because the grass was soaking. My feet felt cold in my inadequate slippers. I arrived at where the stone still lay, slightly askew. Something was wrong. The trench Morgan had dug was full of water and floating on the top and around the immediate area were bones, rib bones, a femur, tiny bones, perhaps from hands and feet. I put my hand to my mouth to stop myself from crying out. This was a burial plot and what Morgan had been trying to dig out was a head stone. What had we done?

I heard a sound, a movement behind me. I turned and there he was, the man from last night. He waved his arms and shouted, yet there was no sound coming from his mouth. I took a step back, lost my footing and slid down into the trench. Freezing water came up to my waist. I cried out. My legs gave way and I almost collapsed. My hands grabbed the sides of the muddy trench. Under my feet I could feel the hardness of bones. The water seemed to be sucking me in. I screamed Morgan's name. The man seemed to be calling on something. And then I heard them. The crows were flying from out of the oak, from the fields, from everywhere. There were masses of them. I was stuck. I screamed until my throat was raw as the crows descended and in no time they were covering me, wings flapping, their beaks pecking into my flesh, while the water sucked me further down into the trench.

I cried out as beaks found soft skin. They were on my head, arms and hands. I ducked my head but my face was too close to the water. By now there were so many birds and the weight of them was pushing my head further towards the pool. Frantically I pushed up against them. Useless. Suddenly my face was in the freezing water. I wanted to gasp yet knew if I took a breath my lungs would fill and I would drown. Air was running out. I had no strength left for the fight. I was going to die here. Maybe I had always known that. I felt my life draining from me, the blackness coming upon me as my lungs were at bursting point.

Something changed. A muffled crack in the air. The weight lifted. I was drifting. My head somehow came up and took a lungful of air, gasping in shuddering fits. Arms were pulling me out and I lay on the ground soaked through, bloodied, shivering, crying, gasping, but I was alive.

Morgan and I moved into a hotel in York later that day. We would sell the cottage. Thank God Morgan had found me. He'd seen the birds first and took his air rifle out to scare them away. Then he had seen me, arms flaying above the waterline.

We've been back in London three months now. We only returned to the cottage on the hill once, to remove our possessions. The garden was a swamp. The cottage stank of decay and we worked fast to get everything out. Water was seeping through the downstairs floorboards, threatening to flood the place. We left without a backwards glance.

# Giddy With It

## Mandy Huggins

On Saturday mornings we coveted satin flares and smock tops in Chelsea Girl; twirling feather boas until neon-bright plumes spiralled to the floor; testing plum-pout lipsticks on puckered lips. We'd claim a window seat at the Wimpy Bar and order milky coffees served in smoked glass beakers; then bitch about the girl with the Linda McCartney hair, and wave at the glam-rock boys in their platform boots from Daisy Roots.

But in the afternoons we were the band: we became Voodoo Velvet. Words encircled our world, chewing biro ends as we wrote our songs, scattering loose-leaf lyrics across your bed. We doodled stars in the margins, hearts and arrows, flowers strewing petals – he loves me, he loves me not.

We made drums from dented Quality Street tins; the drumsticks fashioned from pencils tipped with plasticine. I play-play-played those battered drums until I was giddy, and you strummed an old guitar rescued from the skip; that wreck-necked guitar with only five strings.

You taped it all on your dad's reel-to-reel; my unsure voice, the dum-dum-thrum of the plasticine, our hesitant laughter and the slip-slide-scratch of the steel strings. We borrowed your brother's singles and played obscure B-sides turned down low, writing new words to the old tunes; singing our cosmic lyrics over sixties beats. And then we'd dance to the radio, snake-hipped and slender-wristed, until we were as dizzy as spun candy floss.

We'd stretch out on the rug with bottles of Coke and your mum's ham sandwiches; your Bolan hair a crazy tangle and my pale-sky jeans embroidered with palm trees and flowers.

Then one Sunday morning your brother found the Lou Reed LP we'd scratched, and he took the guitar and smashed it in half. I could hear tears in your voice when you told me, and I bit my lip until I drew blood. But your tears weren't for the guitar. He'd taken the reels too, twisting and stretching the tapes until they were all destroyed. You were breathless with the pain of it; I could hear it in your throat.

We still wrote our songs after that, but we never sang or played again, and our doodled hearts were wrapped in barbed wire. The Linda McCartney girl started coming into town with us, but you didn't tell her about the band, and we stopped going back to your house. We spent Saturday afternoons wandering along the seafront and following the Bowie-boys around the arcades. When my dad got transferred to York we wrote for a while, but I never saw you again.

Years later I'd tell people I used to be in a rock group; that we wore velvet flares and glitter on our cheekbones.

'Songs? Yeah, of course we wrote our own songs. Band members? Just the two of us; me and Chrissie. We were giddy with it all. We could have gone places, you know?'

# On Crosby Beach

## Judith Wilson

On Crosby Beach, where the mud is soft and deep and the sands fine and grey, locals know to watch the encroaching tides. Water can rush from behind or flood three miles at lightning speed.

A child might die with no cry heard, skinny ankles sinking fast.

And all the while, container ships sail back and forth on Liverpool Bay, gracious rectangles atop a winking sea.

Not today. My husband and I have just one thing on our minds. Only this:

'Ha. There they are, the buggers!' Charles has hopped the stone steps, already striking out from the promenade.

The tide it's way beyond, no hint of seven-knot currents, or the maelstrom of sand and brine the mariners used to fear. A shy sun slants our two o'clock beach.

He lays hands on the cast iron body form, pink palms on cold barnacles.

Charles is amused, I can tell. He's wanted to come for years.

'Take a picture. I'll stand next to it. Hi mate, how are you?'

It's a man; naked in all his glory. Antony Gormley's, to be precise. I raise my phone, frame the shot well and tap the focus square. I want to take a good photo, the light perfectly fine, his happy memory of our day. I do five.

Charles poses accordingly. All around us are day-trippers, each picking a life size figure, embracing and hugging and dressing them up.

In the distance: the skeletal forms of Burbo Bank Wind Farm.

Charles doesn't know what else I see as I hold my phone. I spy a boy, not a man.

I've visited before. When Gormley's 'Another Place' arrived in 2005, my parents brought me here. The installation, it was the talk of Merseyside. The three of us stood immobile like the sculptures on a freezing November's day. It was spitting sleet. Natasha and Finn were with me, cantering about. We'd come for a weekend to visit my parents.

Charles was otherwise engaged; a work event, if I recall.

One decade ago these body forms were less weathered, but the barnacles and variegated sheens have multiplied since then. Even so, it was a shock to see the one hundred, strung out like streetlights on the tideline, gazing relentlessly to sea. Three kilometres. A trained athlete could run that distance in ten sharp minutes.

Really? Are you sure?

Anyway, we hadn't stayed long. My father was suffering a bad cold. Later that month it went to his chest, delivered pneumonia. The children soon got bored. Crosby isn't pretty, not like the Cornish sands they knew. I'm not surprised they were restless; I felt it too.

It's the landscape of my childhood.

We had buttered crumpets for tea. Later, I vomited quietly in my parents' floral bathroom. Wiped my lips on the corner of a lilac towel.

I have no sickness today, though. I'm a decade wiser and Natasha and Finn have flown the nest. They've both finished university; we're so proud of them. My parents are gone, and our house is silent during term-time. I've things to do, my JP duties, my charity. Charles is busy at his work; I understand.

It was a whim to drop by en route from the Lake District, his idea.

'Let's view Gormley's masterpiece. Let's visit Tate Liverpool. Let's book a play at the new Everyman.'

How could I refuse? Charles sees life in culture.

(He was born and bred in Oxfordshire; he rode to school on a bicycle and his sister, she had a horse. The sun shone often. It was different for him.)

On Crosby Beach, today it's Spring Bank Holiday. I couldn't deter Charles.

There's an ice-cream van in the car park and for a crazy moment I want a 99, creamy vanilla and chocolate flaking my tongue, perhaps raspberry sauce. Instead I say: 'I heard they're numbered. Is there a 55? Find your other half.'

We have the time. We paddle. The figures stretch one kilometre to the sea.

Vandals have sprayed Seaforth Radar Tower south of the beach; it's redundant, has been for years. I ask Charles if he rates its chunky silhouette, but he dislikes the concrete, the breezeblock.

It was built in the Sixties. We used to picnic in its shadow on the sands. My parents, and I.

On Monday morning, back home, I sit at the kitchen table. I've made tea.

I've the newspaper spread out. Charles has returned to work, regaling his office pals about the mountains we've climbed, those Gormley forms. Just brilliant!

'Hello.' I can't help it; the words pop out.

The boy, he's sitting in silence, wearing a striped T-shirt and a pair of blue shorts. His sandaled feet dangle not quite to the floor; his hair is tousled. I have no fear. Only this. Can he see me?

I don't think so. He's not looking up. In his hands a toy car, it's metal and green, with elongated flanks and miniature axles. He places it on the table, revs it, weaving between jam pot and vase. His hands are precious inches away, scabby knuckles, pale skin.

'Why so long?'

He ignores me. What did I expect? He's humming quietly, and the sound stirs a memory so deep I wince. I keep my body taut - afraid he'll leave. Or that I will cease to see him - whichever is the truth. But he sits on. And I have time to gulp his sandy eyelashes, the high cheekbones and the childish knobble at his knees. Oh my, they're grubby! I ache to clean them.

How old? Eight? Nine?

'WHY SO LONG?'

My voice starts loud and I fear my anger will startle him, so I taper to a whisper. Whoa. I need to calm, shut my eyes, a few deep breaths. This moment, it's too precious to waste. My fingers are hard on my eyeballs. I open up.

He's gone.

I rustle the paper out, read a paragraph. The typeface swims in another language. I put the newspaper down. I stare into the garden, where the rain spatters quietly. A lone pigeon flutters in the apple tree.

Charles and I have had our moments. I can't lie; I've found the children's departure difficult, it has brought a void. We book many weekends away, he suggests them and I acquiesce.

'The Minnack Theatre – let's try it. Hamlet in the rain!'

'The Edinburgh Festival Fringe, always fancied it.'

'Glyndebourne – what's not to like?'

Mostly, we follow through. Occasionally, I stay and he goes; God knows what he does, two nights alone at the last minute, in a 'luxury' country hotel. I don't ask. He always returns. Mondays are usually fine.

And after that very first appearance, the boy is around a great deal. He joins me in the kitchen, when I'm alone. He arrives at varying times and on alternative days. Sometimes, he's already waiting when I push open the door. In the second week, he got into bed beside me one night, when Charles was late from work. I ventured to cradle him; stopped. A month later, he sits in my car. I see him in my rear view mirror, when I've ceased concentrating on the road.

I've decided not to speak. He's happy. I know that.

There's no need for words.

The forecaster was emphatic.

'Wall to wall sunshine this Bank Holiday: perfect day-out weather.'

My mother listened to her radio switched loud, the sounds trailing high above sizzling chops in the pan. 'We'll take a picnic. Crosby Beach. Tomorrow.'

And so we did. She made sandwiches, cheese and pickle, salmon paste, and I wrapped Fondant Fancies in greaseproof paper. My father was the jolliest, always loved a 'Good Day Out.' We packed the tartan wool rug, a flask and our ball, shuttlecocks and racquets. Last weekend, in the garden, I'd beaten both my parents at badminton. We'd drunk lemonade.

The sun arced high in the late May sky and up above was grey-blue, like watercolour swished through milk. We sang all the way in the car.

On Crosby Beach there was a crowd; families like ours, kids on Choppers, and dogs all around. We ate our lunch and kicked the ball a bit. I asked if I could paddle; my father came too, and then, perhaps a little bored or fancying a nap, he left me at the water's edge. My mother waved from afar, a stick insect on a scarlet rug.

'We'll shout when it's time to go. Watch out, the tide rolls in fast.'

I knew that. They'd told me before. I trained my eyes to the sea.

'Hello.'

There was a boy a few feet off, dipping a plastic bucket in the muddy swirl. He was staring at me. His shorts were wet from wading. He held a blue metal spade, its handle long and wooden.

'Have you got your own? Find it – come back.'

It was an order, but I was happy to oblige.

My mother had a beach bag permanently packed, and I was sure within it I'd discover my spade. I hadn't used it these last two years. It was red, plastic, its edges pitted. I returned sharpish. The boy was still alone, hunting for shells.

'It's too busy here.' I acted like I knew everything. 'We need more space.'

I pointed to the distance. To my left, the fuzzy outlines of the Wirral shimmered across the dingy water, but I didn't care about that. I had in mind a solo spot, where we could play alone.

'Up there – where the crowds stop - let's dig further away.'

He nodded OK, and we walked. He was younger than me. I didn't ask where his mum and dad were, if he had brothers, sisters, or a baby in tow. I didn't question anything and nor did he. The sun was hot, the water sparkling and we had a task.

He wasn't local. His voice was soft, lilting, from far away. I enjoyed being the boss.

'I'll dig a hole. You can stand in it. Then it'll be my turn.'

We found a peaceful part with no one around, and laboured fast and long. I wished I wasn't wearing shorts and a T-shirt, that I'd tucked my swimsuit beneath a cotton dress. A hot breeze puffed the beach, swirling ripples on the sand.

I directed and he dug. I paced dimensions; he dug more. Soon the pit was deep enough to stand. We both tried. I lorded it, hands on my hips, and far away, I saw the crowds like coloured ants on stone. The water was flat as kitchen foil. The Isle of Man ferry crept across Liverpool Bay.

I spied the North Wales hills, undulating up and down and far away. 'D'you have a watch?'

He asked it. His arms were chestnut brown and bare; but I had a Timex with a black leather strap, this year's birthday present, my tenth.

'Sure I do.'

'Take it off. Give it to me. I've an idea.'

Since we visited Crosby Beach, Charles hasn't suggested more outings. He's so busy at work he has trips of his own; a few nights in Paris, a whole week to New York.

'Want to come? It'll be a boutique hotel. Nothing cultural, promise.'

I swill his words around, thinking. It would be nice. But I have my JP schedule; those committee meetings won't chair themselves, the funds won't amass without someone to direct charity events. I smile and shake my head.

'You go. I'll be all right.'

I have the boy to keep me company. If only he'd arrived sooner, when Finn, the second to depart, had packed for university. Things might have been better.

Charles and I, we might still be friends.

On Crosby Beach, that bank holiday, I listened to the boy's instructions.

'Stand in the hole. Hold your watch tight. I'll run back to the crowds.'

I nodded.

'I'll raise my arm. Start timing. I'll race as fast as I can.'

'And then?'

'Your turn.'

I trained my eyes down the beach. I watched the boy pace carefully, back to the families and the dogs. The sea twinkled and shifted. The sun hid behind a cumulus, returned brighter than before.

The boy raised his skinny arm. I cracked an imaginary starting pistol.

'Ready, steady, go!'

The return run took longer than we'd guessed. I waited twenty minutes. The sand in the hole sucked at my feet, squeezing tight like pincers. Minute by minute his wiry frame came into view. But by the time he was flailing on the wet beach, panting like a mad thing, the warm wind was gone and the sky pencil grey. I was glad to climb from the hole.

'I should go.'

'We agreed – your turn next.'

Something in the way he said it; I couldn't disobey. And besides, I was two years older; a foot taller, my legs stronger. I wanted to beat him.

'You're a girl. You can't.'

I left my Timex in his sweaty palm. I had no thought for my parents. When they saw me they said: 'Are you ready to leave, love? We need to pack up the car!'

I shook my head.

Ready to race, I trained my eyes back to our special place. Was it there? Was it here? In the gathering haze, soft and wet, the sky was whale grey. I couldn't see him at all.

I couldn't hear him shout, 'Ready, steady, go …'

I raised my arm anyway and I began to sprint. I ran.

Ten minutes in, my bare soles sensed water, not beach. At first, the tiniest splash, no longer sand particles spraying my calves. Faster, I must go faster. My eyes were focused on the distance, but I couldn't see the boy.

Instead, steely sea overlapped my ankles. Cold. It was icy.

I thought of the boy waiting, and I wanted to beat him.

I needed my Timex.

I only –

I stopped and looked back, squinting for my parents. In the shadow of Seaforth Radar Tower, the day-trippers were gathering bags and children, a multi-coloured patchwork swiftly on the move. Between them and me, sudden ribbons of sea. Between the boy and me, another secret swirl. Beyond that was sand, solid and wide and grey, my comfort.

'Coming!'

I wanted my Timex. I'd run faster until I reached it. I'd win.

Yet the further I ran, the harder, the wetter, the deeper …

My father, he was careering fast, I heard his raw and panicked voice before I saw him. He was a big man, once athletic, not for years. But he'd found me. He'd got me. I was waist high and my feet lifting clean off the sand, when he scooped me up, screaming loud.

Several men, breathless, were running close behind.

'You silly girl, stupid! Angry! I'm so angry!'

Angry? The big man, my Daddy, he was crying.

I don't know why I couldn't get the words out. Why I couldn't admit to the boy in the pit. I thought of the water sucking my feet. It was my fault. His game.

My idea. It would be sucking his feet, too. The water was everywhere.

I don't know why, I don't know why, I don't know why.


The week Charles leaves for New York, I book a day off and take the train to Liverpool. The boy comes with me. I see him down the corridor; he's picked an aisle seat. There's a delay; we stop unscheduled for an hour at Crewe. I read my book.

He stares out at the willow herb on the tracks, sprouting violet and green. He's still with me as I change trains, journey on to Waterloo. This time, he stands the whole way, forehead pressed to the window. Perhaps he knows he's coming home. It is October. It's too cold for him; he's still in shorts and striped T-shirt. I want to wrap him tight, my wool coat over his narrow shoulders.

We walk together to the marina, just a few metres apart. Very few day-trippers are here. It's a Tuesday. Everyone is in work or school and has something else on their minds.

We step beyond the dunes and onto the beach. And today the tide is way out, the water stretched so far it is almost lapping Wales. The wind turbines twirl to the breeze. I'm not lonely because the boy is here. He loves Gormley's ghostly men, I can tell. He makes faces, waves his hands. His knuckles are still scabby, skin pale.

Soon, he stands beside me, and for the first time he looks up. I return his gaze.

'I'm sorry,' I say.

For the first time, I'm able to frame the words.

He doesn't smile or acknowledge me. I stare again at his sandy lashes, his tousled hair. Freckles sprinkle his nose.

'I'm sorry.' Here it is again. This time I whisper it.

I shut my eyes. When I open them, the boy is far, far away and wading deep.

The sea laps his shoulders. I want to shout 'Stop!' But it's too late for that. He stands close to Gormley's furthest figure, puts up a hand to hold on tight. I see his eyes locked on the horizon, alongside those stone one hundred others.

They stand so still. The water swirls and foams, then it roars.

The boy doesn't look back, and then he's gone.


On Crosby Beach, where the mud is soft and deep and the sands fine and grey, locals knew to watch the encroaching tides. Water could rush from behind and flood three miles at lightning speed.

A 10-year-old girl was saved, Spring Bank Holiday, 1972.

A boy drowned with no cry heard, skinny ankles sinking fast.

No witnesses came forward.

# Lobsterfest

## Angelita Bradney

'Get down on your fucking knees!' ordered Chef, 'And get out any-thing that's half-edible. We don't want to be short for Lobsterfest.'

Reluctantly, I knelt beside the sack lying open on the kitchen floor. A fruity, rotting smell rose from inside. Some of what was in there was recognisable as carrots. The rest was little more than mush, in a palette of black, white and green. Looking at the squidgy mass made my stomach heave.

'Can I use rubber gloves?'

'Nope.' Chef turned away.

I nearly made a V-sign at his back.

Little over a month ago, a summer job on Jersey, in the Channel Is-lands, had seemed appealing. Live-in kitchen staff/waitress at a beach-side hotel. Good weather, accommodation provided, no experience necessary. At the start of the holidays I'd set off with my backpack and a heightened sense of my eighteen-year-old independence. The five-hour ferry journey from Weymouth was long enough for me to feel on a real adventure, each swell of the sea taking me further from home and the flat I shared with my mother and her new boyfriend.

'You don't mind having the box room do you?' they'd said when we moved in. 'After all, it won't be long until you'll want your own place.'

Arriving on the island, I'd taken a bus from the ferry port to the hotel that would be my refuge for the next three months. The address was 'La route de la baie' which sounded French and exotic. I got down from the bus and, as it drove away, I looked around and gasped. I was at the edge of a vast, sweeping curve of sand, gleaming and flat as new plaster. The sea glittered in the distance. And just across the road was the hotel. There was an outside area with a brown-and-white striped awning and palms growing in pots. A blackboard read: coffees, teas, cappuccinos, espressos. Ice-cold drinks. Fully air conditioned. Hung over the patio chairs were blankets to protect the guests from the sea breeze as they enjoyed the view.

Four long weeks later, looking down at the rotten carrots, I was under no illusions. My job could be part of a horror-behind-the-scenes hotel documentary, or even featured in a piece on modern-day slavery. On the other side of the kitchen, Chef slammed plastic containers of pre-prepared food down on the counter, ready for the microwave. He insisted on being called 'Chef' as if we were in a top restaurant, instead of a place where the uneaten chips on people's plates were tipped back into the fryer to be reused.

Just as he disappeared into the pantry, Katrina, one of the waitresses, came through to the kitchen with a broad smile on her face.

'Five pounds tip!' she trilled.

I shook my head in warning but it was too late.

'That fiver belongs in here!' Chef shot back into the kitchen, shoving a tin at her chest.

It probably wasn't an accident that he brushed her boob with the back of his hand. Katrina silently dropped the note in the tin. In theory, the contents would be shared out every night between Chef and the rest of the staff. In the whole time I had worked here, I had never seen any money from the tin. Breathing through my mouth, I moved closer to the sack of what used to be carrots, and rolled up my sleeves.

Late afternoon, the lull between tea and dinner. The long rays of the sun reached across the bay, entered the hotel and splintered in golden shards on a large tank of water that stood in the hallway. I gazed through the glass at more than a dozen live lobsters. They had arrived earlier that day. Their bodies were a rich brown, burnished with orange, their eyes like tiny black berries. Around their mouths, small appendages like whiskers worked furiously. They seemed oblivious to the rubber bands around their claws. In the office, I knew that new menus were being printed. 'LOBSTERFEST' they read. From tomorrow, there would be a promotional fortnight for the local delicacy. Chef had created four new lobster recipes especially. The smell of sweat warned me that he was approaching. He stood beside me, rubbing his hands together in front of the glass. He was unusually cheerful.

'Look at those babies,' he said. 'A chance to do some real cooking, at last.'

'You don't really boil them alive, do you?' I asked.

He looked at me contemptuously. 'Course. Why?'

'Seems a bit cruel...' I tailed off.

'Add some slices of lemon and a bowlful of Jersey Royals - lovely.' He pressed a fat finger to the glass, leaving a grey smudge. 'Wipe that off, will you?'

I gritted my teeth and picked up my cleaning cloth.

'This week and next,' continued Chef, 'I need you and the girls to be on your best behaviour, no cock-ups.'

I nodded. We'd already had the pep talk that morning. One of the regular staff had told me that Lobsterfest was the most profitable time of year.

The dinner service was in full swing. Apron on, I ran back and forth from the kitchen to the dining room, hot dishes scalding my hands. My feet hurt and my hair stuck to my neck. Plates clashed, Chef shouted, the service bell rang never-endingly. In the dining room, table nine were complaining about the wait. A group of men on table twelve were on their sixth bottle of wine and making lewd comments whenever I was in earshot. I bumped into the other waitresses as the kitchen door swung, and swung again. Dirty glasses piled up at the bar. Chef shook the tips tin in my face – I dropped in the coins I had just picked up. At some point I realised it was late. Tables were starting to empty.

I gathered up the stained cloths. I could now hear the background music in the dining room – pop songs reinterpreted with panpipes. The bar tender counted up the takings. The last table was vacated, its inhabitants staggering out into the night. Now it was time for the damp cloth, the bleach spray, emptying the slop bucket. I swept the floor, then mopped until I could hardly straighten. Soon I was the last one on duty. Chef and the other staff had left long ago. I turned out the lights in the dining room. Exhaustion hung off me like a blanket. In the hallway the receptionist was watching a Polish TV channel, the sound turned low. I paused by the tank where the lobsters were perambulating slowly, oblivious to their fate. When did they sleep? I mounted the back stairs and collapsed into bed.

The next day was the first day of Lobsterfest. I sent my clawed friends a silent 'Hello,' as I passed their tank in the morning. No one ordered one for breakfast. I waited on tables for three hours, counting down the minutes until my mid-morning break. For once, nobody stopped me as I hung up my apron and sprinted out of the kitchen door, past the bins, across the road and onto the beach. The sky was the colour of milk. I spread my arms as I ran across the sand, hoping that the breeze would slough away the greasy smell that clung to my clothes and hair. I headed to the furthest point of the beach from the hotel. It took me a good ten minutes.

Here was a jumble of rocks which, many years ago, had tumbled down into the sea's frothy grasp. The lower boulders were studded with limpets and curled up sea anemones, small and shiny as spat-out sweets. There were good footholds and I clambered over the pools of sea water where creatures hid and waited for the tide. Presently I came upon a boy perched above a particularly large rockpool. He had a bucket and an orange fishing net. As I approached he looked up.

'Shh!' he frowned, 'You'll scare the lobsters.'

'Sorry,' I said. I didn't like to push past, and besides I was curious about what he'd said, so I lowered myself onto a rock opposite him.

Slowly, he took his net and moved it into the water, then twisted his wrist and brought it up with a splash. He peered at it. 'Nothing,' he said, and sighed.

'What are you fishing for?' I asked.

He looked up at me. His nose was covered with freckles. 'Lobsters of course.'

'Do you get lobsters here?'

'Yes,' he declared. 'I've only caught baby ones so far, but one day

I'll get a big'un.'

I looked down into the water. Seaweed sprouted from the rock faces, together with a colony of limpets. Shadows moved in its depths, perhaps just fronds of weed waving in an invisible breeze. The boy lowered his net again. Then he jerked it out and sunk it into his bucket.

'Got one!' he exclaimed.

'Can I have a look?' I said.

He nodded. I clambered around the pool until I was next to him. He pointed down into his bucket. There were something in there, swimming round and round. It was barely half the length of my little finger, almost invisible due to its transparent shell.

'It's a baby lobster,' said the boy.

'Are you sure it's not a... a shrimp sort of thing?'

He nodded vigorously. 'It'll be my pet,' he said. 'But only 'til we leave the beach. Now if I caught a big one, I'd take it home with me and look after it.'

'Well I hope you find one someday,' I said.

Over the rocks a voice called.

'Time to go,' said the boy. He picked up his bucket carefully.

'I've got a lobster too,' I said. "Several, in fact.'

I don't think he heard. He just disappeared over the rocks. It was time for me to go as well. I clambered back and strode toward the hotel. The gulls cried overhead. They seemed to be saying, 'Go, go, go!'

Go where?

'You're late,' said Chef.

I looked at my watch. 'I'm not sure if I am,' I said. According to my watch, I was a minute early.

'Well you fucking are,' he snarled. 'Now get those tables ready for lunch!' I looked across the dining room. Used napkins from breakfast lay over the tables like crushed birds.

Maybe I'd had too much fresh air, but I found myself snapping back. 'Why are you always so nasty?' I said, 'How about saying 'please' for once.'

He said quietly, 'You'd better watch your fucking mouth.'

I wanted to reply but could only come out with stammer noises.

48

"You think you're over for a holiday? Lying around on the beach, a bit of work when it suits you? I know your type,' he went on.

The unfairness hit me in the chest. I found my voice again. 'I work all hours of the day,' I said, 'I've hardly even been to the beach.' My voice was turning into a whine. 'You take our tips, speak to us like we're dirt...'

Against my wishes, tears started to gather in my eyes. I wiped one away quickly. Chef took a step toward me. I looked around. Where were the other staff? There was no one to be seen. I could see the pores on his nose and flakes of skin in his bristling eyebrows. I took a step back.

A voice came from the doorway. 'Excuse me, when are you serving lunch?'

An old couple were standing there. It was the woman who had spoken. She wore a cardigan and a sun-hat that looked as if it had seen better days. I had never been so glad to see a customer. Chef was unable to recover his composure.

'Lunch at twelve,' he barked.

'Thank you,' said the old man.

'Are you all right, dear?' asked the woman.

It took a few seconds before I realised she was talking to me. I shrugged, unable to reply in the affirmative.

'You should treat your staff better, you know,' she said to Chef. She turned to her husband and took his arm. 'Come on.'

I could see Chef's jaw clenching and unclenching as they left. A vein stood out on his forehead like a worm. Then he walked out and left me amongst the empty tables.

Lunchtime. The dining room was busier than usual. In the kitchen I laid down the dirty dishes I was carrying and prepared to go back through.

'Hold it!' It was Chef. 'I've got a job for you,' he said. He beckoned.

I followed him out of the kitchen into the hallway. He stopped at the tank of lobsters. My heart sank.

'Thought you'd like to learn how to cook properly,' he said.

The lobsters were doing a slow dance in the water.

'Pick one,' he said.

I looked around. No sweet old couple to rescue me this time. 'I don't know how.'

'Just stick your hand in!' He made as if to grip my arm.

'Ok, ok,' I shrank away from his touch. Feeling like there was a gun to my head, I plunged my arm into the water. My fingers closed around one of the hapless beasts. I pulled it out and held it away from me, dripping. Its back curled resentfully. It was surprisingly heavy.

Chef jerked his head and I followed him to the kitchen, my heart thumping. On the cooker, steam rose from a large pot of water which spat and growled. Chef took up a knife and cut the bands around the lobster's claws.

'Now, drop it in,' he said.

I felt sweat breaking out on my forehead and under my arms. 'What, now?'

He nodded.

I stared at Chef pleadingly.

His face was impassive, but in his black eyes I thought I saw a glint of satisfaction. The lobster wriggled. My breath was coming fast and shallow. Bubbles detonated in the pot.

'Hurry up!'

I dropped the lobster in. Boiling droplets splashed up like pin-pricks on my skin. There was a hissing noise, a bit like a scream. I dared a glance inside. Through the bubbles the lobster was whipping frantically. Chef clamped on the lid and stood holding it, triumphant. I fled.

I would have liked to hide in the toilets for the rest of my shift, but the kitchen was busy and I couldn't let the other staff down. After ten minutes I crept back in. Chef was waiting. The dish was ready. He hadn't let anyone else take it.

'Table three,' he said.

I looked down at the plate. The lobster lay like a blistered hand on a layer of bright green lettuce, surrounded by lemon slices.

I didn't do anything then and there. I worked into the evening as normal. More lobsters were cooked. I did my duties, spoke little. Kept my face stony.

My alarm went off just before five am. I'd spent a wakeful night. My bag was packed. I'd lose the week's pay, but I didn't care. I crept down the back stairs in the darkness. The reception would be closed; the morning staff not due for another hour. It was a shame for Katrina and the others; no doubt Chef would take his anger out on them. But I'd ruin his Lobsterfest. The hallway was silent, save for the bubbling of the filter in the lobsters' tank. A faint light from outside illuminated the surface of the water.

I stopped by the tank and fumbled for the sack I had taken from the kitchen the previous night – hopefully it would be strong enough. As I plunged my arm into the cold water, goosebumps rose on my skin. Quickly, I picked up the lobsters, one by one, and transferred them gently into the sack. When I had finished there was water all over my clothes and the floor. Someone else would clean that up. A clicking and popping sound was coming from the lobsters.

'Don't worry,' I murmured, 'We'll soon be out of here.'

The fire exit from the kitchen opened with a clunk. I swung the sack of lobsters off the ground and passed through. The door slammed shut behind me.

I ran down the beach, my ankles twisting on the dark sand. The sack was heavy and my bag bumped on my back. There was the tang of salt and seaweed in my mouth. Blood pounded in my ears and unseen shells cracked under my feet. Far out to sea, I could see the lights of fishing boats under the first glimmers of dawn. Panting, I reached the rocks where I had met the boy. I lowered my bags to the ground and pulled off my shoes and socks. I could clearly see the glints of water in the rockpools and the white surf where the tide was climbing the beach. I picked up the sack and pulled it into the sea, wading out as far as I could. I pushed the sides of the sack down until the lobsters were almost able to climb out. Then I coaxed each one over the edge, swiftly pulling the rubber bands off their claws. When I had finished the water was well above my knees and the lobsters had started moving out to sea.

With my remaining bag, I jogged towards the road. There would soon be a bus to the ferry port. I wanted to shout with joy, and I did, crying like a seagull high into the cool air. I looked back towards the horizon, where the distant mass of France would soon be visible. I'd always wanted to go there. The sky was lightening to pale gold. It was going to be a clear day.

# Black Dog

## Julie Hayman

I got my dog when her previous owner didn't want her. The phone rang and my friend said she had a friend who was looking for a new home for her dog - would I have it?

'What's it like?' I asked.

'It's black,' my friend said, 'About the size of a coffee table.'

'Is it good-tempered? Is it inoculated?' I asked.

'What?' said my friend.

'You know, has it had its jabs?'

'Oh, oh, yeah,' said my friend. 'The dog's no trouble. I'd have it myself but I've got no time for one. Tell you what, give it a try and if you don't get on with it, bring it back to me, ok? I'd have it like a shot if I were you.'

She meant she'd have it like a shot if she didn't have a boyfriend or family or any friends whatsoever except her, because a dog has Hobson's Choice whether it wants to hang out with its owner.

'What does it need?' I asked.

'I'll give you the food and the basket,' said my friend, 'And you can take it from there. It's easy, the dog's no trouble. Do you want it or not?'

'Maybe,' I said. 'I'll think about it.'

'Come and get it tomorrow,' said my friend. 'I'll make lunch.'

'Wait,' I said. 'Wait. Is it a girl dog or a boy dog? Is it obedient off the lead? Does it pee in the house?'

But my friend had hung up.

I turned up at my friend's house at twelve the next day. The dog was there, black and shaggy and looking a bit like a goat. It was bigger than a coffee table but I could see where my friend was coming from because it was square in shape with a leg at each corner. It didn't have much of a tail, just a little stump, so I couldn't tell if it was pleased to meet me or not. It jumped up repeatedly on its hind legs to say hello as if dancing the Pogo to a song I couldn't hear, rows and rows of creamy-sharp teeth bouncing near my face.

'Down, down,' I said, ineffectually.

'Get down now,' said my friend, swiping at the dog with a tea towel.

The dog sat as if well-trained all of a sudden.

'Here,' my friend said, handing me a cheese roll, 'Eat this. It'll make the dog think you're dominant if you eat first. She went back into the kitchen.

The dog sat stiffly at my feet, its eyes fixed on the cheese roll, as I ate standing up. Drool slid from its lips in elastic strips. When only one bite was left, it leapt up and took it from out of my fingers and I got a blast of hot dustbin breath in my mouth. I made up my mind to tell my friend gently over lunch that this wasn't the dog for me.

'There you go,' said my friend, coming back into the room, clipping the lead onto the dog's collar and handing it to me. 'The basket and food are outside waiting for you.'

'What about lunch?' I asked aghast, as the dog pulled me towards the front door.

'Cheese roll,' said my friend. 'I'll give you a call tomorrow, see how you're getting on. Bye.'

The dog jumped from the passenger seat to the back seat, and from the back seat to the passenger seat continually as I drove home, barking at the dogs and cats and people and trees and flying litter we passed. Once, it banged its head on the windscreen as it jumped, its front paws sliding along the dashboard towards me as we turned the corner, and there was a tussle for control of the steering wheel. I pushed its muscular chest back onto the passenger seat with my left hand, peering desperately through the saliva-flecked windscreen. A long tongue like a bacon rasher flicked out and licked my cheek.

When we got home, the dog let go a long hiss of steaming piss on the doorstep. Then it walked wet pawprints down the hall.

I put the dog's basket by the back door. Then I put a cupful of dried dog food that looked like Sugar Puffs and smelt like Marmite in a washed-out margarine tub on the kitchen floor because my friend hadn't given me any dog bowls. The dog sniffed it and turned away. It found the downstairs toilet and drank from the bowl. We spent the afternoon watching each other. I closed the curtains in the sitting room before it was dark because, after it got tired of looking at me, the dog stood at the window and barked at the flowers and stone ornaments and boiling clouds above.

Tomorrow I'll phone my friend and make her take the dog back, I thought.

With the curtains closed, we both felt drowsy. I tried to watch a bit of TV, but the dog barked any time a phone rang on screen or a woman laughed or anyone spoke, so I switched it off and went to bed.

The dog followed me.

'Bad dog,' I said. 'Go downstairs.'

The dog started pogoing and showing its teeth again. Frightened, I got changed into my pyjamas and jumped into bed.

The dog got on the end of the bed, gave a great sigh like a steam engine, and fell asleep.

I slept in a foetal position because I couldn't move the dog to stretch out my legs.

The next day I rang my friend. It went to answer phone. I rang again; again I got the answer phone. I withheld my number and rang again. Answer phone. The person you're calling isn't available. Please leave a message after the tone. Beep.

'I can't keep this dog. You'll have to take it back,' I said to the machine. The machine beeped again and shut down before I'd finished speaking.

The dog lay watching me, its chin between its paws. When it wasn't bouncing around, it looked tragic, like a caged gorilla. Patient and sad and knowledgeable of human sin.

I took it out into the garden on its lead. That pepped it up. It peed on the grass and I knew that in a matter of days the green blades would singe and shrivel from the concentrated dose of uric acid. The dog crouched, one haunch resting atop my stone faun playing pan-pipes. I tried to see where the pee was coming from, to figure out whether the dog was a boy or girl, but I couldn't get down low enough, and I wasn't sure whether the dog was crouching or cocking its leg: it seemed to be doing both. Once finished, the leg came down, knocking over the faun so that its nose came off and the panpipes broke away. I took the dog back indoors. It started barking loudly at the window, its ears opening, closing, opening, closing, synchronised, as if the barks were coming out of the ears as well as the mouth.

The dog sat at my feet and stared as I ate a ready-made cottage pie with broccoli and cabbage on a tray on my lap in the living room. Its eyes pulsed, its nostrils dilated and contracted and goo dribbled from its chops. I thought about shutting the dog in the kitchen. It inched for-ward and its tongue unrolled and flicked against the cabbage. I gave it the bit it had touched, hoping that would satisfy it and make it go away. I put the tray on the bookshelf while I got myself a drink of water and when I came back the food had gone.

I phoned my friend again and left another message. I thought about just driving the dog back there and tying it to her door knob, but couldn't face the journey with the dog bouncing inside the car like a furry power-ball.

We went for a walk in the woods. At first the dog pulled on the lead but after a while we fell into a rhythm together, the dog walking slower than it wanted to and me walking faster. The dog was all pricked ears and sharp eyes and rippling shoulders and thumping paws. When we got to a clearing in the wood, I unclipped the lead. The dog bounded off into the underbrush. I tracked its progress by the trajectory of ex-cited barks and the sudden flight of birds from trees. The barking got fainter. When I could hear it no longer, I turned quickly and made my way out of the wood by a different path.

When I was so close to the exit that I could hear traffic hissing by on the road, the dog reappeared, panting, its tongue dangling sideways out of its mouth, burrs in its fur and its muzzle stiff with mud. It seemed very happy. It stood in front of me and looked disingenuously into my face. I hoped it didn't know what I'd been up to. I clipped the lead on and the dog led me out of the woods.

We passed a bald man walking a hefty white dog on a lead. The dog had the face of a shark and the man had angry eyes which blinked hello as if issuing a challenge. The two dogs went for each other suddenly with blood-frothing sounds and we each pulled them back, me and the bald man, playing tug of war. Finally the dogs broke away from each other and we walked on. I was trembling from the flash-fight but the black dog's step was jaunty, the stump of a tail lifted in a thumbs-up to the sky.

My friend didn't ring back, and she avoided me at work. I'd see her deep in conversation with colleagues at the coffee machine and, as I approached, her back would turn like the bowl of a tracking satellite dish. She'd zip down the stairs as I came out onto the landing, she'd slide around pillars and accelerate out of the car park facing rigidly forwards.

Dog owners began to notice me on our regular walks, and nod. The tall woman with a hat like a frisbee and a whippet on a lead. The short woman, prematurely white, with a jumpy step and a tangled ball of terrier. The short-legged man in the waxed jacket, cheeks red as a gnome's, who walked a muzzled Malamute. I learned the names of the dogs as the owners chided them: 'Come here, Walter'; 'On with you, Zack'; 'This way, Podge.' I wondered what the black dog's name was. I tried a few out when we got home, when it was comfortable and relaxed licking its paws and shedding fleas on the sofa.

'Blackie,' I called. 'Sooty.'

The dog ignored me.

Pitch. Jet. Snowy.

The dog carried on licking as if deaf.

'Dinner,' I said.

Its head snapped up. It unfolded its legs and started to pogo, there on the sofa.

I bought a waxed jacket, jeans, jumpers, T-shirts, wellies and a rain-hat. Except when I was at work, these were the clothes I wore.

The black dog seemed to need a lot of walks: half-an-hour round the block in the morning before breakfast; an hour's run in the woods each teatime; a sniff through the park each evening. My pace quickened, I lost weight, my cheeks got a permanent flush.

I won't keep the dog, I said to myself, But I will look after it properly until I can get hold of my friend and make her take it back. I rang her each week, on Sunday evenings at seven: she never picked up and I never again tried to leave a message. The dog watched dolefully as I dialled; sometimes it put a paw on my knee as if sympathising. Then we'd go into the living room, shut the curtains and I'd roll a tennis ball along the carpet. The dog would bring the ball back to me, holding it tight in its jaws so I'd have to prise it out of them. Then I'd roll it again. Sometimes the dog bit me, just a little, without breaking the skin, when I took the ball: it was part of the game. We'd play this for an hour or so. Often, when we finished playing, the dog would pass the time by gnawing vigorously under its tail, then drag its hind quarters across the room to empty its anal glands, sometimes leaving a slimy brown trail across the carpet which I'd scrub clean with soapy water.

The dog still slept on the end of my bed every night but it now let me wriggle my feet under its haunches to keep warm.

One Friday evening, the dog found a dead rat under a bush in the garden and ate it. It got ill, waking me at four on Saturday morning, scratching at the bedroom door to be let out. I took it downstairs and opened the back door, standing in the doorframe shivering with my dressing gown tied tight. The moon was howling-bright and the stars fizzed. The dog crouched on the grass peddling its back paws, and foul-smelling faeces ran out of it. Then it vomited, keeling forward on the patio and banging its head on the flagstones. I helped it up and steadied it as it staggered back into the house and flopped onto the kitchen floor, panting.

I rang the out-of-hours vet surgery.

'Dog's name?' they asked.

Dog's name? Dog's name?

'Winner,' I said, after slightly too long a pause. 'I haven't had it long. It looks really poorly.'

Bring it in, they said. You'll probably have to leave it with us for a while.

The dog curled itself on the passenger seat, its head on my lap as we drove the two miles with the windows cracked open to let out the foul smell of partly-digested rotting rat. The vet put the black dog in a cage, shaved its leg and attached a drip there.

'I'll ring you in the morning with an update,' the vet said. 'We'll do what we can. Is the pet insured? Unfortunately, our consultation fees are higher at the weekend. It'll cost about £500.'

I sprang out of bed like a missile the next morning when the phone rang.

The vet talked very fast as if spinning plates, and left me no gap in which to interject. 'There's no change,' she said. 'Winner still has diarrhoea and is still vomiting. We won't offer food until we've got this under control. We're administering antibiotics, anti-nausea pills, and something to line the wall of the gut in case of inflammation. We'd better keep the dog in. I'll ring again tomorrow.'

'Thank you for looking after...' I said, as the line went dead.

I ate my toast leisurely that morning, and left the plate perched on the arm of the sofa while I got another cup of tea and brought in the post from the letterbox and found the newspaper. I superglued the panpipes to the nasally-defective stone faun and then, having not much else to do, watched television all day: re-runs of Friends, mostly. I ate pizza off a tray on my lap at dinnertime, and left a packet of half-eaten Jaffa Cakes open on the floor while I went off to the loo.

The next morning I raced downstairs when the vet rang.

'No change,' she said. 'We'll keep your dog in again tonight.'

'It's not my dog,' I said.

'Who's paying the bill?' she asked, her voice sharp.

'Oh, me,' I said. 'I'll pay.'

The week passed this way: vomiting stopped Monday; no diarrhoea on Tuesday; Wednesday the dog was offered food, which was refused. The vet added an appetite stimulant to the smorgasbord of drugs and informed me that I now owed just under two thousand pounds; Thursday, the dog still wasn't eating; Friday, no change to report.

That week, I went to work and came home and felt continuously out-of-sorts, as if I wanted to do something but couldn't decide what. I bumped into my friend in the corridor at work, there being no time for her to duck into a handy room to avoid me.

'How are you?' she said coming forward, beaming as if delighted to see me, touching my arm in a friendly manner.

'How are *you*?' I retaliated, brushing off her hand and walking by. So now I had no friends. It was a relief.

Each evening when I got home, I spent time looking out at the rain-studded garden, watching the sky scud by and the dog's diarrhoea on the lawn get mushier by the day. I'd get my ready-meal out of the fridge and into the oven and then, twenty minutes later, out of the oven and onto a plate and sit with it on my lap, my eyes running across the telly, my heart tapping away the time until the next morning and the next update.

On Saturday morning when the vet rang, I said firmly that I wanted to visit the dog. The vet agreed that I could visit at eight o'clock that evening. I could pay my bill to date at the same time, she said, though the dog wasn't well enough to come home.

The vet stood disapprovingly over me as she opened the cage door. The black dog looked like a rucked-up rug thrown over the cement floor. There was a dish of untouched chicken beside its head, a cannula in its leg. I didn't know what words to say to make the dog get up and be itself again. I knelt beside it and it raised its head a little and sniffed at me and its stump waggled a little. I bent forward slowly and kissed the top of the dog's head and its ear and muzzle, and an understanding moved between us and mingled in our breath.

'Please come home,' I whispered, 'Please get well,' and something sparked inside me like a flint struck in a fairytale.

'We'll let you know,' said the vet as I left, her eyes chips of mica in granite.

I drove straight to the woods, parked the car illegally, and jogged along the footpath. I hadn't run at all since I was a child, but I wanted to then. Something leapt in me that had been long confined. Mizzling rain lifted vapours into the air which curled richly into the honey-comb chambers of my nose: the pong of poodle shit, the on-heat ooze from a Beagle bitch, potent sniffs and whiffs of Staffie urine. The syrupy-scent of horse chestnut sap clung to my skin; the kalei-doscopic aroma of mown grass held the notes of each passing paw; the chiaroscuro smell of badger greased the sharply-creased stems of long grasses. Colours faded and the world became a three-dimension-al olfactory meshwork of notes and trails and sequences of animal thoroughfare. I ran hard, leaping fallen trees, startling birds, jumping fences, ripping through brambles so that I hardly knew where I was. I ran and ran, my legs not my own, lungs burning, mouth gaping wide, my body quivering in delight, panting. I ran through the maelstrom of ecstatic odours until I lost the scent of the one - frightened, timid, gentle, naked - that was mine.

# Eggshells

## Oscar Lopez

I'm on my third bite and then crunch. A tooth, I think, wincing. It must have cracked last night. Then I feel it splinter: it's just an eggshell, the pieces floating in my mouth. I breathe a sigh of relief.

'Everything alright love?' he says.

I swallow - the bits of shell slither down my throat. I force myself to nod.

'Love my omelettes don't ya?'

I smile but it hurts so I keep eating in silence, picking furtively through the rest for other bits of shell. I get up to put my plate in the sink.

'Let me,' he says, grabbing the plate.

I sit down. Now all I can smell is eggs, in my clothes, my hair. While he's turned away, I reach my hand to my face: it still feels swollen, like I've got an egg lodged in my cheek.

'I'm going out with the lads tonight,' he says, scrubbing the plate. 'Footy's on.'

There's another bit of eggshell stuck between my teeth - I try to pick it out with my tongue. After some slobbery manoeuvring I manage to remove it. Then there's the metallic taste of blood and I realise the tooth has come out too. It's sitting sharp on my tongue.

'Cat got your tongue?' he asks, setting the plate down.

I watch the suds slide into the sink and disappear. I look back at him, muscles rippling as he grips the scourer. I nod again and look away as I swallow the tooth.

# Doolally Tap
## Sarah Edghill

It wasn't really great weather for the beach, but she couldn't stand being in the house any longer. They were cutting tiles for the bathroom floor, using an electric drill that shrieked like a scalded child.

'We'll be out of your hair by Friday!' the man in blue overalls had reassured her.

That was two weeks ago, but there were still walls to be plastered, windows to be painted and no end of plumbing wizardry to be carried out with overflows, S-traps and single handle mixers.

The dog didn't fancy the beach either, and sat resolutely on the slipway that ran into the sand, forcing her to drag him down by the lead, his bottom carving a trail in the dirt.

'Don't be ridiculous,' she told him. 'You'll get friction burn.'

By the time they reached the sea wall at the far end, the drizzle had turned into proper rain and water was worming its way down her collar and into her boots. The dog looked up at her, pleading for mercy.

'Don't make me feel guilty. You're the reason we're out in this!' she told him, irritably.

The sand they'd crossed had been left pock-marked and muddy by the deluge, so she walked back along the road, exchanging self-deprecating greetings and raised eyebrows with the handful of others who were braving the elements.

She was worried she'd made the wrong decision about the taps: maybe she should have chosen chrome? Brass effect looked fine on the basin, but seemed ostentatious over the bath. Perhaps she should have gone for a mixer tap, rather than a monobloc?

'It's too new-fangled,' she told the dog.

To her left the beach was deserted, the sea and sky both the colour of pewter, the waves foaming as they died on the shore.

As she approached the house she could hear the squealing of the drill. The pile of building rubbish outside the back door was enormous: misshapen slabs of breezeblock, metal rods, rusted strands of wire mesh, blocks of white insulation. A dusty mound of floor tile offcuts had been tipped onto the top since she left the house. She stopped to take a closer look.

'They're very pale,' she pointed out to the dog. 'Almost white in this light. I wanted that floor to look marbled.'

She pushed open the door and walked briskly along to the bathroom, her boots leaving muddy splotches on the floor.

'I'm not sure about these tiles,' she announced in the doorway. 'Actually I think they're quite wrong. I will need to go to B&Q and find something else.'

The two men stared at her, mouths open, foreheads knitted into frowns of disbelief.

'The thing is, we just can't spend any more time on this!' the man in the blue overalls started to say. 'We're overdue at the next job, and...'

She shook her head, swatting him away. 'Those taps aren't right either, they'll have to come off again. I've decided I want chrome after all.'

# Saturday Nights

## Diane Simmons

I almost don't mention it at school. I don't want a repeat of the piss-taking I got for liking Wings.

'Did you see that John Curry on the telly yesterday – winning the gold?' I ask eventually.

Sandra grins at me. 'It were brill. The three of us should go!' she says, flicking Pat's arm to get her attention. 'They have a DJ at the ice rink, Saturdays.'

We're not there half an hour before Sandra's off up the back seats snogging some boy with dirty finger nails. I glare at any other lads who look like they might approach and Pat and I have a right laugh trying to stay upright, clinging on to each other for support.

I'm soon tons better than Pat. I love it. I don't even mind the cramp in my toes or the manky café that smells of stale fat. And I manage to get round the rink on my own, even get to the centre where all the posers are hanging out doing spins and jumps. I don't abandon Pat at the barrier for long though. I take her hand and guide her round the rink, will her to enjoy it as much as me.

Sandra decides to go to some nightclub the next week, but Pat and I don't miss her at the rink. I have more fun than I ever would at any disco. As usual, there are boys eyeing us up, but Pat doesn't bother with them and keeps ogling some older guy with David Essex hair.

'Will you chase after him for me?' she asks. 'I'd never catch him.'

It takes me four goes round the ice and two falls before I crash into the barrier next to him. 'You need to learn how to stop,' he says, and winks at me. 'I can show you, if you want.'

'My friend wants to know if you'll go out with her.'

He looks me up and down, slowly moves his eyes away from my bust. 'Which one's she, then?'

'Over there – the pretty one with the blue jumper.'

'Perhaps? Send her over.'

I skate slowly. I can feel him still staring and I'm desperate to stay upright. I shake my head at Pat. 'Sorry, he's already got a girlfriend.'

At registration on the Monday, Pat picks her nails, shrugs. 'Me and Sandra thought we'd give that new nightclub a go next Saturday. You up for it?'

I feel like I've been slapped. I get why they want to go, of course I do. I can picture them next week dressed up in their black stilettoes and the slinky dresses they bought from Miss Selfridge, dancing, scanning the room for boys, plotting who they'll get off with for the slow dance in the dark. I envy them the dark. But I'd rather be at the ice rink, gliding along to a soppy song, having the chance to hold another girl's hand.

I couldn't do that at a nightclub.

# Food of Love

## Dan Brotzel

We met at a farmers market, standing by a stall offering South African beef jerky and biodynamic Stilton. I laughed as you hoovered up all the samples, feigning gourmet appreciation to cover your greed.

On our first date, we saw Super Size Me at your beloved arthouse cinema, followed by Belgian waffles and ice cream. The next few months were a blur of weekends in bed, fortified by home-made café au laits and Cumberland sausage sarnies.

The day you proposed, we sat against a windbreak on the beach, one cold February morning. Remember? We shared a tray of vinegary chips to wash down the little bottle of warm Cava you'd bought along. (I've still got the plastic fork somewhere.)

The allotment. Years it took to get it, then we found chard and squash were about the only things we could grow that didn't get eaten away. But all those wonderful picnics we had there, drinking stewed tea from your granddad's old Thermos flask. And all those excruciatingly ingenious marrow recipes...

After I gave birth to the twins, you surprised me with a feast of all the things I'd had to give up while pregnant: bubbly, Brie and prawns. Mealtimes took on their happy routine: slow-cooker casserole on a Saturday, roast on a Sunday, hot chocolate after school concerts, your eccentric 'power salads' in summer.

But of all the meals that make up a marriage, I never saw it coming to this: vending-machine Hula Hoops for me, and nil-by-mouth for you.

# Robin
# (The Handle of
# a Child's Bucket)
## Diane Beaff

**From: Tcampion@supernet.com**
**To: Slogan@supernet.com**
**Subject: Robin**

Hello Shanty,

As you can appreciate, it's been an unimaginably tough summer. The first since Robin's death. I know you've been asked so many times already, even in a criminal capacity I suspect, but I would appreciate hearing any and all details of that awful night yet again.

I just can't reconcile the fact that Robin never mentioned you in all the months you were seeing each other. It's so unlike her. We were very close, as I'm sure you know. You were too old for her and I wish you would have discouraged her interest. Made her realize that at fifteen she was far too young for any serious relationship, especially with someone nearly twenty years old.

You're as familiar with the environs of Robert's Arm and beyond as anyone, and working for Biff Leinoff's logging crew must have required you to drive that road to Corner Brook many times before. So why were you speeding? Why did you have Robin out so late on a school night in the first place? All reasoning escapes me.

Please help me to understand why your life goes on as ever, when Robin's is no more, and any peace for me has been utterly shattered.

I've attached a photo of Robin's Junior High graduation last fall. All lace and ribbons she was, as you can see. Blue was her favorite color. It brought out the sea-colors in her eyes. A sweet, sweet child she was. So full of promise and possibility. An innocent life snuffed out just like that on one of our lonely Newfoundland byways.

I hope to hear from you.

Sincerely,
Tilda Campion


**From: Slogan@supernet.com**
**To: Tcampion@supernet.com**
**Subject: Robin**

Dear Mrs. Campion,

I can only say that it was beyond devastating for me to wake up in the Stephensville Hospital last April and be told that Robin was gone. It still seems unreal to me.

We really hadn't been seeing each other at all. Robin was my sister Carla's best friend, as you know, and I guess it was inevitable that we'd get to know each other somewhat.

I have to say, once again, that I don't remember much of that night at all, except for the thick fog that still seems to smother everything about it. I don't even know for sure when we set off for home, or even any friends we might have seen in town.

I'm so sorry for the loss of your daughter and for whatever part I played in it. I am, it seems, very much at fault, though accepting blame can never be enough, I know. How could it be? If I could say or do anything to ease your pain, I would do it gladly. I know you will never be able to forgive me. I will never forgive myself.

Sincerely,
Shanty Logan

**From: Tcampion@supernet.com**
**To: Slogan@supernet.com**
**Subject: Robin**

Shanty,

Accidents like this can diminish ones memory, I know. But surely there's something, however trivial, that you can bring to mind. It would mean the world to me to be able to somehow align myself with Robin in her final hours. Regrettably, I'm torn with the injustice of her life being snatched away from me, while yours, spared for whatever reason, goes on as usual. Your suffering is great, I have no doubt. But there is no way it can possibly compare to a mother's loss of her only child.

I have so little of Robin's essence with me now. Somewhere I read of a man who kept a beach ball filled with a loved one's breath, his wife's, I think. Someone who'd been lost to him. I have nothing along those lines beyond a lock of Robin's hair, a soft sand-colored swatch from the day she was born.

There are, of course, simpler items, like the cobalt blue toothbrush she never managed to get back in the holder. It's still lying on the bathroom counter where she left it all those many months ago. That's all I have. Beyond an infinity of memories that play continually in my head, always coming to rest, if that's the right word, on her bruised and broken body.

I have attached here an old snapshot taken down by the harbor when she was about three years old. We'd only just lost her father to cancer. I hardly ever go out anymore and so I've buried myself in old photographs these past months as something of an escape. This one caught my eye. That oversized cap she's wearing, I guess.

I had only just remarked the morning of the accident that she looked quite piqued, as though she'd lost sleep a night or two. Her eyes were hollow and dark. She shrugged me off and set off for Central High as usual. Carla was waiting by the bus-stop. I could see her from the kitchen window. I know, of course, that Carla was with you and Robin that awful night, but she has thus far refused to talk to me.

That was the last I ever saw of my darling girl. You can't imagine what that has done to me. So I feel certain that there's something, however mundane, that you can add to that day. Perhaps you owe it to Robin's memory?

Sincerely,
Tilda Campion


**From: Slogan@supernet.com**
**To: Tcampion@supernet.com**
**Subject: Robin**

Dear Mrs. Campion,

I will try again to give you as accurate an account of that night as I can.

As I've said, I fetched the girls from school to drive down to Corner Brook for a Harry Martin concert. That stretch of road is a lonely one at the best of times and a dense fog had rolled in by the time we headed for home. I don't now recall the exact time, but it had to be close to midnight, maybe later.

We weren't dating, Mrs. Campion, and if Robin implied otherwise, I don't know how she got that idea. I never led her on in any way. Carla can vouch for that. It was my understanding that Robin had your ok for this trip, so I can only say that I'm sorry I didn't follow up on that.

After the concert, we started directly for home. Moose always seem to find that stretch of road, so I can tell you, without hesitation, that I was not speeding. I just have no other specific recollection of what happened on the drive.

I only remember waking up in Stephensville, or it may have been Port aux Basques, days later. I wish I could help you in some way through this terrible loss. Maybe one day you will find it in your heart to forgive me.

Sincerely,
Shanty

**From: Tcampion@supernet.com**
**To: Slogan@supernet.com**
**Subject: Robin**

Shanty,

There may well come a day for forgiveness, though that's not an option for me at present, I'm afraid. There are days when I can barely get out of bed. I hear Robin's voice in a crashing wave or the wind in some seaside pine. She's in the hum of our old T.V. set in the den.

Sometimes, when I'm in the check-out line at the Red and White, it's as if she just popped back in for another box of Smarties. She always did that. And then someone will tell me they're ever so sorry for my loss and I'm pulled right back into the nightmare my life has become since she died.

I've attached another photo taken a year or two after the last one. That green plastic bucket she's holding there? She built a thousand sand castles with that. In fact, she used it just last summer to collect seashells. She'd gathered an exquisite mass of periwinkles, mussels, clams and sand dollars and had gone back to the car for a towel to haul away even more when an errant wave wrenched the whole thing out to sea. Sand-pail and all.

Another rogue wave, it seems, has ripped her own gentle self from me, now, body and soul. I can hardly bear it.

Tilda Campion

**From: Slogan@supernet.com**
**To: Tcampion@supernet.com**
**Subject: Robin**

Dear Mrs. Campion,

As you probably know, Shanty is off with Biff's outfit on the logging harvest over by White Bay. He'll be gone 'til at least the middle of September.

I don't usually look on his computer, but he's been so low lately, what with Robin and all, that I thought I'd have a quick shifty and so I ran across your emails. Robin was my best friend in all the world and I know it's far worse you being her mom, but everyone is crushed from losing her.

My brother never wanted you to know, but for his sake, I have to tell you the truth about that night. Shanty's told you about going to see Harry Martin in Corner Brook, but that's just the half of it. Mr. Martin was playing, but Shanty didn't take us down. Robin and I went with Blaine Jernigan, a senior at Central. He'd told us about some party near the docks and I talked Robin into going with me.

Parents don't like to see these things. I know my mom didn't. But Blaine does a lot of meth. If you want a hit, he's your go-to guy. Me and Robin got into that about a year ago. At least I did. Robin started up just a few months ago. Anyway, Shanty got wind of things, as big brothers sometimes do, and he drove down to get us.

We started for home around midnight, just like he says. That's a pretty lonely, stretch of road and Shanty knows better than to speed when there's moose around. He was at the wheel and Robin was in the front seat. But she wouldn't keep her seat-belt on and round about where the 430 goes up north there by Deer Lake, she started opening her door and slamming it shut over and over again.

Shanty was afraid she meant to jump out, so he reached across to pull her back. But she just kept laughing and laughing and slapping at him. He must have lost control of the car before we could stop. I don't remember what happened after that. Just that the roadside marsh got closer and closer in slow motion. And then I must have blacked out.

Shanty said you'd suffered enough having lost your only child. So he asked me not to tell anyone. About Robin or the meth. No mom wants to hear her baby girl is a meth-head. But Constable Harcourt can tell you the whole truth. Maybe that's why you've never asked him for details and he was hesitant to give them.

Shanty's the best big brother anybody could have, Mrs. Campion. He's been like a dad to me since our own left when I was about five. But sometimes his heart is just too big for his own good. So, I'm begging you, Mrs. Campion, don't do this to him. No more pictures. No more guilt. He doesn't deserve it.

Carla Logan

From: Tcampion@supernet.com
To: Slogan@supernet.com
Subject: Robin

Dear Carla,

I know Shanty's still over by White Bay, so I hope you'll be reading this in his stead and can pass it on. It's been a lengthy, strange and very difficult struggle to come to terms with your last letter, which is why I've waited so long to answer. I did indeed check with Constable Harcourt and to my ever-lasting devastation and heart-break, he confirmed all that you said.

I am shattered. Absolutely gutted. I no longer have reason to doubt your brother's motives or actions and so I can only fall back on the good man you say he is. Please convey to him my deepest apologies and let him know, if you can, that the forgiveness he thought he needed from me, I now ask of him.

Best,
Tilda Campion


From: recohen@supernet.com
To: Tcampion@supernet.com
Subject: Robin

Dear Tilda,

Having missed you of late, I am deeply concerned for your welfare. Moreover, numerous phone messages I have left you have thus far gone unanswered, as have those of your many friends and acquaintances in the congregation. Nor have you answered your doorbell. You are in shock. I do understand and appreciate that. But please allow me, as your pastor, to be of some comfort and support at this very difficult time, when Robin's passing is still so raw and unbearable.

We do not always see the workings of Divinity in our lives, in the many strange coincidences or seemingly inexplicable tragedies that so often befall us. We can only turn our own lives and the lives of our loved ones over to a Higher Power and trust that there is some pattern, some Divine reasoning that may, in time, comfort our souls and give us peace.

The loss of a child is particularly odious and debilitating, and we must all strive prayerfully to accept Divine Will, even in the direst of circumstances. Regrets are inevitable even in a life well-lived.

We are none so pure that we can escape the sting of remorse, or of things better left unsaid. But a burden of guilt serves only to nullify and oppress the life spirit of we who must soldier on.

So it is now with Shanty's death in White Bay.

We may never have all the answers. A 'logging accident' seems overly simplistic and painfully non-specific. It gives us no solace, no measure of discernment or acceptance, more especially if we look to the past instead of struggling to face the future. So I must tell you again that you do not have to bear your burden alone.

Sincerely,
Reverend Cohen

# Front Cover Down

### Shirley Golden

You were of average height but grew taller with each telling. Your hair was burnt-orange, the tone darker. No one used the word ugly, but thick-set, hooded eyes, and a nose that looked as if you'd been in a fight.

Someone said you were a musician and others recalled hearing the string notes of a cello, straying from your open windows. Artistic, tapered fingers. Soft. Delicate. No, that couldn't be right.

The dead girls hadn't time to go cold before they came looking. Reporters scribbled furiously, ink like slaver. They'd seen husks worse than this. They packed around the mother and father, who bowed their heads in a wreath of sadness over their remaining child.

'No, you weren't a friend,' they said.

One woman claimed you'd held open the post office door on a frosty morning when her arms were packed with parcels. You were softly spoken but didn't say much; of the gruff tone of your voice, she was adamant. She couldn't remember specific words, only the buckle of your teeth.

They waited for the landlord to unlock. They wanted proof of duvets and spoons; signs that someone like you had, at least, to live like everyone else. They clustered into the entrance to discover a half-filled glass of water, a lumpy sofa, shrouded in a blanket, a crime novel – front cover down. No cello. No TV. A coffee mug with dregs, and yes, there were spoons.

It was a suspected electrical fault.

But nothing to indicate how you'd be the one to push past bystanders, a towel masking your mouth, and charge into smoke plumes to save a child, who knew you by sight alone.

# Honeysuckle Happiness Hospice

Ian Tucker

Honeysuckle Happiness Hospice
Tilebury Chase
Wessex

Miss Leonora Dalmis
Dr Stephanie Dalmis-Jackson
Mr Bede Dalmis
Mr Rawlton Dalmis

26 May XXXX

Dear Leonora, Stevie, Bede and Rawlton,

I am dying. You are my only relatives.

I have moved to the above address so my remaining days can be spent bothering nurses and looking at flowers. A succession of doctors (five) has told me that I will be dead before the end of the month. I have decided there is no point in obtaining a sixth opinion.

To entertain me in my final days I have amended my will. It is attached. Read it carefully.

I do not intend to be an unconscionable time a-dying. Consequently, if you choose to act, act fast. My current net worth stands at £26-Million.

Any further updates will be posted to my website
www.richterminalcurmudgeonlybastard.com.

You might like to keep an eye on it. Leave me messages there if you want. I will not respond to telephone or email.

Don't visit me.

Yours sincerely
Sir Broderick Dalmis


## Last Will and Testament

I Broderick Alnwick Seth Dalmis (Sir), currently of Honeysuckle Happiness Hospice, Tilebury Chase, being of sound mind but failing body, do hereby declare this to be my Will and revoke all previous Wills or testamentary dispositions made by me. I appoint Meryon Davis of Davis & Lornabaker Solicitors to be my Executor.

After paying all debts owed by me at the time of my death, and on the conditions set out in this Will, I bequeath my Estate as follows:

I leave my entire Estate in equal shares to each of the following (my "Heirs") who shall have completed, by or before the time of my death, the conditions set out in the schedule to this Will:

My niece Miss Leonora Dalmis, who has avoided ever doing a day's work by being beautiful;
My niece Dr Stephanie Dalmis-Jackson, who has worked every day of her life and never said or done a brilliant thing;
My cousin Mr Bede Dalmis, who has always excelled at ephemera but failed in everything else; and
My nephew Mr Rawlton Dalmis, whose lifestyle has left him in sore need of an inheritance.

Remainder, Mr Meryon Davis as Trustee for my cat Furborg for as long as Furborg shall live and upon Furborg's death The Dalmis Foundation for the Prevention of Cruelty to Cats, a charitable foundation to be founded by Mr Davis on such terms complying with the laws of charities as he shall think fit in his absolute discretion, without anyone interfering in that discretion or trying unduly to influence or annoy him or generally get in his way, howsoever, whatsoever, ever.

In witness whereof, I have signed this Will on 26 May XXXX in the presence of the Witnesses below:

Broderick Dalmis:
Squiggle
First Witness:
Different Squiggle
Second Witness:
Dissimilar Squiggle


The Schedule:

The conditions each of my Heirs must comply with before my death shall be:

1. To set fire to an object belonging to each of my other Heirs at midnight on Balinty Tor.
2. To upload a video of him or herself completing condition 1 onto my website along with a description setting out the details of how he or she complied with condition 1.
3. To send me a postcard such that it reaches me before my death stating my mother's job before she got married.
4. To run naked along the full length of T'mas Broad, Tilebury from the Ship Inn to Walling Street.

**Email 09.13 27 May XXXX**
**From Leakitten@Incite.com**
**To  SirdontyouforgetitBroderick@richterminalcurmudgeonlybastard.**
**com**

Uncle Brod!
Wow you're so mad! [smiley face]  Love the gag.  So funny LOL. But
so pervy too!! Running naked down T'mas Broad? Soooo wrong, uncle
Brod – no way!!! Bad Uncle Brod!
Go on – don't be silly. You've always been such a sweet darling. It's all
a big joke, right? So sorry about the cancer thing – ignore those doc-
tors, their always wrong yeh! Chin up. I'll come down next weekend,
see you then. Busy just now – new fashion thing I'm doing. So cool!!
Tell you later.
Lots love
Leonora.


**Email 09.14 27 May XXXX**
**From       SirdontyouforgetitBroderick@richterminalcurmudgeonlybas-**
**tard.com**
**To Leakitten@Incite.com**
**AUTOMATIC REPLY**

I am busy dying. I will not read or respond to your email. I can't be
bothered.
Sir Broderick


**Email 09.31 27 May XXXX**
**From Leakitten@Incite.com**
**To RawltonDalmis@Everon.com**

Hi Rawly-Crawly,
Did Uncle Brod send you that funny will thing? Hes finally lost it.

Barking, LOL.

Whats he up to? Is he really dying? I mean really really? He's been saying it for ages. And whats with those loony conditions? Cant be legal? The nutters always doing jokes but this is just weird.

Did you get it too?

Lea

**Post to Forum on www.richterminalcurmudgeonlybastard.com**
**9.59am May 27 XXXX**
**Stephanie said:**

Dear Uncle Broderick,

I have received a very odd letter which claims to be from you. It enclosed what looked like a fake will someone has put together. I think it is a joke but it is in very poor taste. I don't want to worry you but I think you should know that someone might be pretending to be you. You may have heard of identity theft. They often target old and vulnerable people, particularly if they are beginning to be forgetful and having mental problems. If you want any help with it please do let me know. The letter says you have moved into the Honeysuckle Happiness Hospice – I do not know if that is true because the letter appears to be a hoax, however if you are there I am pleased. They are very good to older people there. I'm in Taunton these days so can come over to see you if you like.

Your niece, Stephanie

**Email 11.01 27 May XXXX**
**From RawltonDalmis@Everon.com**
**To Leakitten@Incite.com**

Hi Sis,

Yeah, I got it too. Damned odd. The old man's brain's addled I reckon.

Too much Gin. I'll probably be like that when I'm his age. Anyway I gave that place a call – they wouldn't put me through to him and his mobile's off. He is there. They said so. So I called that lawyer-jerk he uses. Bloody Welsh bastard wouldn't tell me anything except that he drew up the will yesterday and he says its serious.

I'm thinking we should go down there and sort this out. But bloody inconvenient at the mo. Really busy and I haven't got time to drive down just to give the old man the satisfaction of tweaking my tail. I reckon he wants some attention and thinks he deserves it if we want his money. You got time to pop over and see him?
R


**Email 12.17 27 May XXXX**
**From Leakitten@Incite.com**
**To RawltonDalmis@Everon.com**

Hold on a sec! Its serious?!!! The lawyer guy said that? No way! Lawyer's don't go round fibbing – you have to be a right bore to be a lawyer – I met a few in my time and had to run away in the morning before breakfast. Their sooooo Dullllll!

But if its serious – we could be in for loads of money here, couldn't we? Don't know bout you but I never thought the old fruitcake would leave me anything. He can be such a deletive expleted. But if this is real we could get the lot?

The way I read it (dont quote) the money gets divvied up between whoevers' prepared to do his silly little tasks in the next couple of days. Well – one is running naked down T'mas Broad. No way boring old Stiffy or Uncle Beedybug are doing that right? You and me? Different story.

Maybe we should be in on this?

**Email 14.58 27 May XXXX**
**From Dr.Fitzgerald@Honeysuckle-Happiness.com**
**To DrSDalmis-Jackson@Wessextrust.nhs.uk**

Dear Stevie,

Good to speak to you again after so long. We should meet up some time.

Further to our discussion on the phone, I can confirm that Sir Broderick Dalmis is indeed a patient of ours and that unfortunately he is suffering from numerous inoperable metastatic tumours which we expect to prove terminal.

Sir Broderick is now on palliative treatment. Although he remains lively and in full command of his faculties, we do not expect him to live many more days. I'm afraid there is no doubt about this. Sir Broderick demanded that the tests be run several times and I (and quite of few of my colleagues) confirmed the conclusions to him.
Although this is a personal and private matter, I feel I can tell you as you are next of kin and are professionally qualified to fully understand the facts. I am sorry if this comes as shocking news and if there is anything I can do to help you or the family at this difficult time please do let me know.

Regarding your question about a will, I'm afraid I don't know. Sir Broderick's lawyer did visit him yesterday and Sir Broderick has given instructions that he is not to receive visitors or phone calls. He is a strong minded gentleman and I'm afraid we cannot ignore his instructions.

Kind regards,
Alan Fitzgerald

**Email 16.23 27 May XXXX**
**From RawltonDalmis@Everon.com**
**To Leakitten@Incite.com**

You may have a point. Streaking down T'mas Broad – done it before, do it again. Once lost a bet to Old Derry and had to run all the way home from the Ship, starkers. Not seen you do it though – Lea the Tit'mas Broad. Ha Ha. Way you're stacked, you'll be bouncing all over the place on those cobbles. I wouldn't need Brod's money – I'd make a mint selling tickets.

Burning stuff on Balinty Tor. Strange imagination the old boy has. You know the Tor's haunted? Some wizened ghost's supposed to appear at midnight. That's why Brod chose it, I reckon. Swap you something of mine for something of yours to burn. How'll we get something from Stevie and Uncle Bead?

What the hell was his mum's job? No idea. That was granddad's first wife right?

**Post to Forum on www.richterminalcurmudgeonlybastard.com**
**7.39pm May 27 XXXX**
**Inconvenient Millionaire said:**

Stevie - the letter is genuine. I wrote it. So is the will. I am not vulnerable or forgetful. If you don't want my money, forget it.

**Email 20.43 27 May XXXX**
**From Leakitten@Incite.com**
**To RawltonDalmis@Everon.com**

Hey! Just had a call from Stiffy!! Shes sooo pissed off. You seen Uncle Brod's website yet? He's been leaving her rude messages!!!! She was all over it, saying he's mad and we should have him committed or something and wanted us to gang up and challenge the will and stuff. I said it was Brod's money and if he wanted us to run naked down T'mas Broad that was up to him. She so hated that!! I had to mute the phone so she couldn't hear me laughing.

Anyway I think the games on. I've got tomorrow off – can you make it to Tilebury. Ship Inn 7pm? I've got a towel I nicked when I stayed with Stiffy last year. That'll do for burning. Uncle Beedy lives near Gloucester right? You're coming that way – drop in on him and get us something on the way. Bring the tent – we'll go on to Balinty Tor after. two birds one stone.

Deal Bro?


**Email 21.19 27 May XXXX**
**From RawltonDalmis@Everon.com**
**To Leakitten@Incite.com**

Deal. Got the tent. See you then. I'm reckoning naked running's gonna need at least 5 pints.


**Postcard (mallard duck).**
**Delivered by hand at the Honeysuckle Happiness Hospice, morning 28 May XXXX**

Dear Broderick,

I tried to visit but was not permitted in to see you. I was told this was on your instructions. Although I could feel hurt I am mostly concerned for you. You do not need to cut yourself off from your family like this. I will pray for you.

I do not know what to make of the will you sent to me. Your mother, of course, was a singer and magician's assistant with the Entertainments National Service Association during the war. I have photos of her in my family history album. As you mentioned her, I brought it down in case you wanted to see them.

I would have preferred to talk with you about the old times. However, as you would not see me or answer the phone I am leaving this postcard instead. I will stay in Tilebury tonight and can return tomorrow if you wish. If it would help, I could ask the local priest to come and see you. You may find some solace that way, if not in your family.

Your cousin
Bede


**Post to Forum on www.richterminalcurmudgeonlybastard.com**
**2.36pm May 28 XXXX**
**Inconvenient Millionaire said:**

Bede. I don't like God-botherers. If He and I are destined to meet soon I shall have the good grace not to waste His time with prayers and hair-splitting. You are right about my mother. Warning to the rest of you – Bede's got a head start.


**Text 4.11pm May 28 XXXX 'Rawly' to 'Lea'**
Unc Bede not home. Can't find anything to take. Have to try later. See you 7pm.


**Email 17.28 28 May XXXX**
**From Enquiries@TileburyNewInn.co.uk**
**To DrSDalmis-Jackson@Wessextrust.nhs.uk**

Dear Dr Dalmis-Jackson,

Just to confirm your booking tonight. I'm afraid the only available option is the Four-Poster Room which makes things more expensive. However, there are two beds in there and I noticed one of our other guests was Mr B Dalmis (room 4) – is he a relation? If so, we could put you together and save you some cost? Let me know.

New Inn - bookings


**Text 9.59pm May 28 XXXX 'Cousin Leonora' to 'Stiffy'**
Stephanie you cow. Bring our clothes back!!!! Lea


**Text 10.07pm May 28 XXXX 'Cousin Leonora' to 'Stiffy'**
Now Stephanie!!!! We're in Rawly's car. Lea


**Text 10.13pm May 28 XXXX 'Cousin Leonora' to 'Stiffy'**
This is war, you bitch. All my other clothes are in my car and the keys in my coat. If you don't bring it back now I will never speak to you again.


**Text 10.21pm May 28 XXXX 'Cousin Leonora' to 'Stiffy'**
Thats it. You'll regret this.


**New Inn "Suggestions" box. Note left late evening 28 May XXXX**

Please write your suggestion here:

I do not appreciate the behaviour of your other guests. They may think it is funny to leave articles of a man and woman's undergarments and a scarf on the handle to my room but I do not. It is your responsibility to police the behaviour of your clientele. Also I believe someone has been in my room. An album of family photographs is missing from my bag.

Bede Dalmis – Room 4

We are grateful for your feedback.


**Post to Forum on www.richterminalcurmudgeonlybastard.com**
**2.01am May 19 XXXX**
**Stephanie said:**

Dear Uncle Broderick,

I attach a short video shot with my phone this evening on Balinty Tor. You will see it starts with a picture of my watch at 11.58 and ends at 12.01am. I extinguished the fire shortly afterwards.

You requested an explanation. I came to Tilebury this afternoon where I saw your cousin Bede in the Lounge Bar of the New Inn. I went to reception where I told them I was his niece and asked for his key, which they gave me. Then I went to his room and borrowed the family photo album he had in his bag (which includes some pictures of your mother).

Sitting in my car on Walling Street, Tilebury at about 9.30 I saw my cousins Rawlton and Leonora come out of the Ship Inn. They were unsteady on their feet, wearing long coats and laughing. Rawlton had a large bag which he hid behind the phonebox on Walling Street. When they returned to the Ship Inn, I collected the bag and locked it in my car boot.

Then I walked down T'mas Broad to the Ship Inn just in time to see my cousins emerge together, throw off their coats revealing nothing beneath, and run down the street. A large group of pub-goers emerged from the Inn and pursued them yelling advice. I believe Leonora may have seen me as she passed.

While everyone was looking the other way, I collected my cousins' coats and drove to Balinty, where I climbed the Tor and set the fire. You will see in the video that I consign one of Rawlton's socks, Leonora's tights and one of Uncle Bede's photos of me to the flames. In return for the album I have left one of my old scarves and some of my cousins' clothing for Bede.

You will get a postcard tomorrow.

**Post to Forum on www.richterminalcurmudgeonlybastard.com**
**6.59am May 19 XXXX**
**Impressed Old Codger said:**

Stevie – brilliant! Never thought you had it in you. I'll die laughing. Video reminds me of camping there as a boy. I trust Rawlton and Lea will make sure the whole village's ready and waiting for your naked dash. Must have been a thousand people watching when I did it. Midsummer fayre 1968, I think.

**Email 07.19 19 May XXXX**
**From RawltonDalmis@Everon.com**
**To DrSDalmis-Jackson@Wessextrust.nhs.uk**

Stevie. Lea is furious with you. So am I, but I'm handling it. Peace meeting. Meet me in the Lounge of the New Inn? Rawls

**Email 07.55 29 May XXXX**

From DrSDalmis-Jackson@Wessextrust.nhs.uk
To RawltonDalmis@Everon.com

Rawlton. I'm having breakfast there now. Come join me, if you're decent. Stephanie.

**Daily Activity Sheet 29 May XXXX.**
**Officer Recording: PC Mogul 65227 Tilebury.**

0004885759
Time of incident: 04.15am
Description of Incident: Elderly male observed unclothed on T'mas Broad. Apparently running with a twisted ankle. Overtook man with brisk walk but was unable to convince him to stop until he reached Walling Street. Man identified himself as Bede Maurice Dalmis and requested to be taken back to his room at the New Inn. Produced key for same. 04.25 arrested B Dalmis - indecent exposure. Drove him to Tilebury station 04.35. Provided police issue paper clothing. Mr Dalmis explained that he had fallen on broken cobbles outside Ship Inn. Particularly keen that I record this location. Reason for exposure not adequately explained. Mr Dalmis referred repeatedly to a challenge set for him by his cousin. No previous record. 05.13am Holding cell 3. 08.40am Verbal caution.
8.45am Released.
Entry completed: 08.55am 29 May XXXX

0004885760
Time of incident 09.05am
Description of Incident: Returning Mr B Dalmis to New Inn following incident 0004885759. Assisted gentleman to his room (4). On return – informed by proprietor of suspicious behaviour of Male (estimated 30-35). Male entered Lounge bar while breakfast being served. Well dressed but badly groomed. Dark hair, bags under eyes. Sat with guest (Dr Dalmis-Jackson, Four Poster Room). Appeared to know

each other. Short conversation. Left lounge together approximately 7.40 and got into his car.

Proprietor not certain Dr Dalmis-Jackson willing. Argument overheard. Also woman in car wearing man's coat, blonde, striking appearance. Dr Dalmis-Jackson did not return to room. Currently, no grounds for suspicion. To check Dr Dalmis-Jackson returns later. Entry completed 09.35am 29 May XXXX

**Post to Forum on www.richterminalcurmudgeonlybastard.com**
**10.51am May 29 XXXX**
**Old Codger Still Quite Impressed Despite Considerable Pain said:**

Stevie – I have your postcard. You are right about my mother. She was only half my current age when she died, you know. They sent me camping on the Tor that night so I wouldn't see her go. Only one task left for you. Nurses taken me off painkillers 'cos my body can't take it. Had to refuse to see a priest this morning. I may be running out of time. As may you lot. Not many more midnights for a bonfire.

**Post to Forum on www.richterminalcurmudgeonlybastard.com**
**12.22pm May 29 XXXX**
**Lea said:**

Uncle Brod. We want to see you. But Rawls and me have been talking and we think you want us to complete the task's first. We think your doing it to make us be more fun. So we're going to do the bonfire on the Tor thing tonight and send you your postcard before we come visit. Don't die on us. Rawls and Stiffy (reluctantly) and me are climbing the Tor now with the tent. Hang in there.

Oh – and if you're reading this Uncle Bede weve got your photos. Stiffy gave them to us, after Rawls did a bit of convincing on her. If you want them back you'd better come get them.

Post to Forum on www.richterminalcurmudgeonlybastard.com
13.05pm May 29 XXXX
Expiring Uncle said:

Get on with it. I can't hack this much longer. You only know how brilliant the drugs were when they take them away. Maybe if you see a ghost up there it'll be mine. Like I saw my mum's. You aren't related to her, of course, and I never thought you had her determination. Maybe I was wrong. Just get on with it.

Post to Forum on www.richterminalcurmudgeonlybastard.com
15.09pm May 29 XXXX
Bede said:

Don't destroy the album. That is our past. Without it all we are to each other is some genes. I'm coming.

Post to Forum on www.richterminalcurmudgeonlybastard.com
19.52pm May 29 XXXX
Alive by the Power of My Mind Only said:

I'm still here. Time is passing me but the clock won't bloody move. Don't destroy Bede's photos. I'm sorry. I never meant that. It was to stop you all being so distant and dull and so feckless. Come on midnight.

Post to Forum on www.richterminalcurmudgeonlybastard.com
20.47pm May 29 XXXX
Rawlton, Lea, Bede and Stephanie on the Tor said:

Don't give up uncle Broderick. The sun has gone down. The fire's lit. It's a clear night. We've all got our sacrifices. Bede's camera's set up. Rawlton and Leonora have written their postcards. Don't leave us till we get to you.

**Post to Forum on www.richterminalcurmudgeonlybastard.com**
**21.03pm May 29 XXXX**
**Rawlton, Lea, Bede and Stephanie on the Tor said:**

Uncle Brod?

**Post to Forum on www.richterminalcurmudgeonlybastard.com**
**21.47pm May 29 XXXX**
**Swearing survivor said:**

Still here. Don't know when I'm awake and when I'm dreaming. The clock moved. I'll not sleep again. Not normal sleep. Raging against the dying light. If only you could swear yourself alive.

**Post to Forum on www.richterminalcurmudgeonlybastard.com**
**23.16pm May 29 XXXX**
**Bede said:**

We saw something Broderick. A white figure passing on the horizon. Silly superstition but are you still there? The others think I'm mad. But I saw something.

**Post to Forum on www.richterminalcurmudgeonlybastard.com**
**23.42pm May 29 XXXX**
**Not a gost yet said:**

Wans't me. come for me maybe not aready yet


**Post to Forum on www.richterminalcurmudgeonlybastard.com**
**0.01am May 30 XXXX**
**Lea said:**

Done it, Uncle Brod. Video uploaded. We're on our way. Watch it and wait for us. Rawly is carrying the stuff back down the Tor, Bede's putting out the fire. Stiffy already went down to getting her kit off in the car. You needed details – Bede had some clothes of ours already; he gave us a glove each and Stiffy gave us each a lipstick from her purse. Rawls and I exchanged store cards from our wallets. Coming now.


**Post to Forum on www.richterminalcurmudgeonlybastard.com**
**0.09am May 30 XXXX**
**lonelyfool said:**

stupid old manm I didn wan tto die alone.


**Post to Forum on www.richterminalcurmudgeonlybastard.com**
**00.59am May 30 XXXX**
**Lea said:**

Hang on Uncle B! We're in Tilebury. Broke sound barrier getting here. On Walling St. Stiffy jumped out at Ship Inn in the buff. Car Door's open – engine running. Rawls hovering over accelerator. Here she comes. Uncle Brod? You still there?


**Post to Forum on www.richterminalcurmudgeonlybastard.com**
**00.13am May 30 XXXX**
**Lea said:**

Uncle B!  Please be there!!!!

**Post to Forum on www.richterminalcurmudgeonlybastard.com**
**00.51am May 30 XXXX**
**Lea said:**

Front doors locked. Rawls slid the car against the garden wall. We're climbing over from the car roof. Can't carry laptop any further.

### Honeysuckle Happiness Hospice - Memorandum of Death

Sir Broderick Alnwick Seth Dalmis died 00.58am on 30 May XXXX in the garden suite. He briefly regained consciousness when his nephew Rawlton Dalmis smashed the window, climbed in and handed him two postcards. At time of death Sir Broderick was surrounded by his surviving family. His last words were, 'Got you together, at least. That's something.'

# Keep Calm and Carry On
## Emily Richards

I've a pad of inspirational quotes – one for each day – stuck to my fridge. My sis gave 'em last Christmas. Big ideas for yer little head, Neil, maybe you'll be inspired and like, leave the house? Princess Angelica, I think, I see your idea and raise it. I'll live that pad, 365 days of inspirationeil. I say that, laughing, but she walks out shaking her head. Probably to give our parents the pity report. Bide your time, Neily, I think. Christmas 2017, show 'em all then, just bide it.

Jan's great. I dance like no-one's watching and it's easy: no-one is. I twat around to Queen, get my hooverin' done too. Next, I live, laugh and love – bit more abstract but fully doable: Terry and I watch Fools and Horses on G.O.L.D and laugh our arses off. Terry's my hamster: I love that furry bastard. I give him double treats as a random act of kindness, no stress. Terry's over the bloody moon.

Feb I have to walk a mile in someone else's shoes. Metaphor, I know, but I'm leaning in 100%. I pick Patrick – homeless fella round the corner, on the high street. Never knew his name before, he takes some persuading but eventually accepts my Doc Martens as a holding deposit; I march his bashed up Cons along the canal. I have a good think about Patrick the whole way, really empathising. I'm practically in tears when I get back, but the bastard's done a runner. Unlucky for him, he picks the shop doorway below my flat to hide in. Lucky for him, I'm still mopin' about his parents lettin' him sleep outside Debenhams, so I say keep the shoes, come for tea.

I do us waffles and beans. Pat wants sausages but I'm veggie, I say. Since I got Terry, I tell him, not got the heart. Pat just eats. I point out the pad on the fridge, explain all, how it inspired today's events. He shrugs, asks what's tomorrow.

Peepin's not protocol, but Pat's a guest, so I check. When you get knocked down, roll over and look at the stars. It's a clear night, I say, let's go on the roof. I been knocked down and looked at stars enough, Pat says. A tinny convinces him. Roof's quiet, Orion's Belt's out, inspiration feels like it's working. Friends AND hobbies, I think, next Christmas Neil, you'll show 'em. You feel any calmer, I ask, more inspired? Calmer than what, says Patrick, I need a piss. You'll need the key, I say. When he slams the door it's the only sound on the street.

Thirty minutes, no return. Don't be hurt Neil, I think, he doesn't know it's the only key. He'll be back soon, no doubt. So I stay lying down in the peaceful silence, wondering whether today is a day when good things come to those who wait or a day to take a leap and trust I'll land on my feet.

# The Birth of Venus

## Stephen Palmer

'It's a matter of discernment,' Andreas told Mel shortly after they met. They were sitting outside a bar opposite the Cathedral, drinking white wine on a bright yet balmy spring evening. 'You must have the strength to decide what you do and don't like and be prepared to stand by it. Because if you think this is culture and have to like it all – understand it all – then you have overload, an artistic short circuit.'

'You mean if the Botticellis don't get you, the Caravaggios will.'

'Exactly.'

It was true. When Mel had first arrived in Florence she'd been dazzled and bewildered. Having marvelled at Michelangelo's Pieta, strained her neck gazing at the cupola mosaic in the Baptistery until she was convinced that the last judgement was nigh, and peered so long at Orcagna's tabernacle that her senses became a swirling arabesque, she began to doubt the here and now. After passing through the Piazza della Signoria and its statues by Michelangelo, Donatello and Giambologna, the blue bronze of Cellini's Perseus made a foreign country of the past and the future another planet. By the time she had suffered the relentless accumulation of Madonnas with child in the Uffizi, her sense of identity was on the verge of collapse.

Mel thought that love must be similar. You need discernment. Otherwise you're left in a daze; the here and now in doubt, the past problematic and the future uncertain.

She knew where she was, of course. The here and now was the rattle of the rails and rumble of the train taking her from airport into the city. But no sooner did she establish the sense of her surroundings; the tourists and their rucksacks giving off an odour of perspiration and scorched canvas, the thinly upholstered seat hard beneath her, than they fragmented and thoughts of England and what Gary had said flooded her mind. Even the clear Tuscan light, the light that bleached her hair a blonde that neither the English climate nor chemicals could achieve, that in the past seemed to elucidate the shape of things and at the same time penetrate to their essence, now dazzled and bewildered her with its brilliance.

Despite this Mel insisted to herself that she knew exactly what the future held. Because what Gary had said was ridiculous. But the steps through which this future was to come into being had become confused. She was to catch the train from Florence to Frankfurt where her wedding was to take place. That much was clear. But then she remembered she first had to go to her apartment off the Via La Marmora. And then to the institute where she worked to say goodbye to her colleagues. But, no, go to the institute first. There's no point humping all of that luggage around.

At the station she queued at the kiosk to confirm the connections to Frankfurt. A man wheeling a bicycle stood beside her.

'Inglese?' he asked.

'Nein. Deutsche.' Mel pushed the hand that was hovering close to her backside away. She remembered how her bottom was black and blue for weeks after she had first come to Italy. Besides, it wasn't really a lie. After they were married and Andreas had finished his doctorate they would live in Frankfurt.

Mel smiled at the thought but what in the past had motivated such a smile crumbled within her and she found her cheeks burning. And there was something she needed to do that she had either forgotten or had yet to enter her consciousness. It produced a vacuum inside her so that her belly was sucked up under her ribs. Guilt, she thought. Because of the kiss. But that, too, was ridiculous. True, it was a very long kiss. The landlord of the pub had to intervene on the grounds, he claimed, that they would soon suffocate each other. Snogging he had called it and that was what it was. The sort of thing fourteen year olds do. If she told Andreas about it he would laugh. They would laugh about it together.

She turned the key and walked into the bare apartment. The relief she had expected at taking her first steps towards Andreas failed to materialise. All her things except for the suitcase she had already packed had been taken to Andreas' much larger apartment. Seeing her home of two years stripped of her possessions left the feeling that part of her life had been stolen from her.

Pre-marital nerves, she thought. If I'd known what going home was going to do I wouldn't have bothered. It had been courtesy. She had little in common with her old school friends these days but as none of them could afford to go to the wedding she had decided to visit. She was surprised to see Gary in the scruffy pub where they used to congregate because it was cheap and no one asked their age. Back in those days Gary was too young even for that establishment.

'Remember Gary,' Fiona said. 'My little brother.'

Mel replied that she did and they had smiled at one another.

She picked up her suitcase, locked the apartment door and posted the key in the mailbox for the landlord to pick up. She would just have time to say goodbye to her work colleagues. Not that she really needed to say goodbye. She would be back at work in two weeks.

She took the street behind the Museum of Fine Art and came out on the Piazza Santissima Annunziata. The suitcase was heavy and Mel would have liked to sit by the bronze fountains where she and Andreas had first kissed and bathed in the serenity of the square but she was short of time.

In the shade of the portico she fell to thinking about how old she would have been when Gary first saw her. Eleven or twelve, she thought. She couldn't remember the first time she saw him. He just seemed to drift into her consciousness. The little brother of a friend. Her first distinct memory of him was after leaving school by the back entrance adjacent to the sports field.

'Look,' said Fiona, 'there's my little brother playing football.'

Mel looked and Gary scored the winning goal. It wasn't a very good goal. The goalkeeper fumbled the muddy ball and Gary poked it in from two yards. Neither Mel nor Fiona were interested in football but they cheered and clapped to support the school and continued watching until Fiona began to moan about the cold.

It was when two boys on mopeds shouted out something not quite obscene at the intersection of the Via Dei Servi and Via Bufalini that Mel realised she was nowhere near the institute. She did not, however, turn back but wondered, as she passed the Cathedral, how she knew Gary's was the winning goal if she didn't stay to the end of the match.

She had no idea where she was going or why she was going there but she followed the Via Dei Calzaioli past the church of Orsinmichele. I went back to Fiona's for tea, she thought. That's how I know.

'We won,' Gary shouted as he burst through the door, 'and I scored the winner.'

'Big deal,' said Fiona.

Mel, who also had a little brother, understood the necessity of this denigration of Gary's achievement but cringed inwardly as she anticipated the reaction of Gary's mother.

'These shorts are filthy. How am I supposed to get them clean?' She held them away from her as if it may have been more than just mud on them.

Mel had realised some time before that Mrs Banks was one of those women who would never be happy. When something bad happened it confirmed her expectations and the good provoked suspicion.

'I'll do my best but don't expect them to be white and don't go thinking we can afford a new pair.'

'It's alright Mum,' Gary said. 'It's not that important.'

Mel came into the Piazza della Signoria. It was here, in order to avoid succumbing to cultural overload, they began listing their likes and dislikes. Andreas had begun by declaring his distaste for Donatello's statue of Judith beheading Holosfernes.

'That's because you're a man,' said Mel.

Andreas laughed. 'Perhaps. But it doesn't matter what the reasons are as long as you have some criterion by which to judge it. You can change your opinion later when you know more but you need somewhere to start.'

And what Andreas said was true. Whereas before she had been overwhelmed, in Andreas's company she began enjoying what she saw, sometimes even laughing as she gave her opinions, no matter how naive, on everything from the Fat Bacchus in the Boboli gardens to Michelangelo's David. Under Andreas' rules it was surprisingly easy to find something to say about everything until they came to the statue she was looking up at now.

The blue face of Perseus was stern and heroic as he held in his outstretched fist the tangle of blue snakes from which hung the gorgon's severed head.

'It's beautiful but I don't like it,' Mel had told Andreas.

'Why not?'

'I don't know.'

Mel dropped the suitcase and took a step backwards. A red heat rushed to her chest as she studied the gorgon's face. The blush spread to her neck as the memory came back to her.

She had gone to visit Fiona but Fiona was in the bath and she had to wait in the kitchen. Fiona's mother didn't look like a gorgon. Except when she saw the book Mel took from her pocket and began reading rather than listen to Fiona's mother haranguing the world.

'What's that you're reading?' demanded Mrs Banks.

It was Simone de Beauvoir's The Second Sex. Mel blanched a little and, not thinking, raised the book so that Mrs Banks could read the title. But of course, she couldn't read the title because Mel was reading it in the original; Le Deuxième Sex. All Mrs Banks understood was that it wasn't English and had something to do with sex. Then she gave a look of which Medusa would have been proud; her face seemed to tighten about her skull and the eyes glared.

'I don't know why you want to read that rubbish. It just puts silly ideas into your head.'

Mel blushed as she was blushing now beneath Cellini's masterpiece. At the time she didn't understand why she was blushing. It's not rubbish, she thought. Even if I don't understand it all. And I'm good at languages.

It was that fluency with languages that had led her to this moment. Bathed in a brilliant Tuscan light, she was surrounded by a city the people of which, the artistic treasures, even the terrible traffic, she considered her own. There was a future with a brilliant and loving husband to look forward to. It was her love of languages that had let her escape people like Mrs Banks forever saying her hopes would come to nothing and gloating when they were proved right. So why was she blushing then and why was she, caught in the Medusa's gaze, blushing now? Because Gary, Fiona's irrelevant little brother of whom she took no notice, was sitting in the corner watching as Mrs Banks heaped scorn on all her dreams.

She turned and hurried towards the Uffizi gallery, checking she had enough credit on her mobile so she could call Andreas later. She knew now where she was going. She walked through the early rooms with their relentless Madonnas with child, passed the Raphaels and Titians without a glance and merely gave a respectful nod to Leonardo's Adoration before stopping before Botticelli's The Birth of Venus. Relief rippled through her at finding what she was looking for; the goddess on a shell, floating on a foam flecked blue sea with her attendants about her. Mel hadn't liked it at first.

'Why not?' Andreas asked.

'It's too pretty. Looking at it for too long would be like eating a whole bag of marshmallows. You'd feel sick after a while.'

But one morning as she was dressing Andreas told her to stop. She was startled by the demand in his tone but his expression of adoration mingled with that of someone who had just experienced a minor revelation reassured her. He stepped forward and Mel tasted his warm tobacco tinted lips on hers and felt her left breast enclosed in the heat of his large hand.

'I've just realised who your breasts remind me of,' said Andreas.

Mel pulled away and smiled, puzzled but indulgent.

'What are you talking about?'

'Botticelli's Venus,' said Andreas. 'Your breasts are like those in the Birth of Venus.'

Mel laughed. 'But you can't see...' she began but her words were stopped by Andreas's mouth covering hers. A hot, passionate mouth that moved over her cheek and chin, down to her neck and chest and on to her left breast.

Mel couldn't resist and she was late into the institute that morning.

She gazed at the painting before her; the goddess on a shell floating on a foam flecked blue sea and the small, plump breast with its creamy white skin and orange nipple. Something warm and tender passed into her own breasts at the memory of Andreas' lips covering them. But you still can't see the right one, she thought as her eyes fell on the long, flowing hair that obscured that part of Venus' bosom. She smiled. I'm going to marry Andreas.

She lifted her suitcase and walked away but not towards the exit. Instead she carried on further into the museum. There was something else she had to see. Past the Rembrandts and the Tintorettos that Andreas loved to the room that Andreas scorned.

'He's superficial. If he was alive today he'd be making pop music and not even good pop music. He'd be more interested in the drugs and the girls than art.'

Caravaggio.

Mel looked for a while at the Young Bacchus and another Medusa, her face reflected on Perseus' shield. But these were not what she had come for. She turned.

'It's disturbing,' she had told Andreas. 'It's almost as if the angel has arrived too late – as if even though he's not going to do it the fact that he would have is going to scar him for life.'

The angel was to the left of the painting as Mel looked at it, its upraised arm illuminated and pointing to a revelatory light on the opposite side. Between the angel and the light were Isaac, stretched out on a sacrificial slab, and Abraham with knife in hand. Isaac's expression is, not surprisingly, one of panic although tempered by the beginnings of hope in the eyes. It seems that, head lolling back, he has seen the light but will only understand its meaning when, lifting his head from the slab as he is doing, he will see the angel. It is not clear whether Abraham has seen either the light or the angel. He still holds the knife to Isaac's throat but his head has turned away. It may be that he has yet to see the angel or, having seen it he is petrified by the artist in the movement that, following the angel's pointing hand, will lead to the distant light.

105

Mel thought the painting was superb but hadn't been able to explain to Andreas why. She understood now as she sensed Abraham's dizzying sense of being halted in the course of an action long contemplated. The same dizzying sense she had experienced when she had kissed Gary. Because it wasn't just a snog. It was much more than that. Neither of them were fourteen and Gary was no longer Fiona's little brother from the moment he said that it was a pity she had left home to live abroad.

'Why?'

'Because I've loved you from the first moment I saw you.'

Mel managed to halt the gasp that threatened to issue from her open mouth but not her belly turning into a swirling arabesque or her bladder filling so that for a moment she thought she was going to wet herself or the airy sensation in her head that the day of judgement was nigh. She put her hand to her mouth as she told herself this sickening sense of exhilaration was simply the result of her vanity being flattered. But as she looked into his face the thought evaporated. She saw that face afresh. It was as if she had never seen it before yet at the same time it was extraordinarily familiar. It was no longer the face of Fiona's little brother, no longer a boy's face although it was the man's face that the boy's face had always foreshadowed. It was the face she had always known it would become and always known she would one day love.

Her heart contracted into a ball and then contracted further as if attempting to force itself into an infinitesimally small point outside of this confusing, frightening, electrifying world. But her body was beyond its control. Her hand moved forward, hesitated, and then reached out to touch his face. She felt his fingers on her lips and then she was in his arms, suffocating in his kisses so that they had to pull away for breath and stare at one another before sinking again into their passion, oblivious of Fiona and their friends until the landlord came and put a stop to it. At which point they did feel like fourteen year olds.

Mel looked at Abraham in his moment of indecision and then across to the angel who was about to make his decision for him. Mel wished she had an angel to make her decision for her. She knew what the painting signified. She was Abraham and whatever she did someone was going to be scarred. But she couldn't tell whether the angel calling her to her rightful destiny was Andreas or Gary.

She turned and left the museum and walked through the Florentine streets. She passed Cellini's Perseus and Giambologna's Cosimo de Medici and Michelangelo's David and Donatello's Judith but they seemed different now; somehow drained of meaning. It's a psychosis, she thought; love. It bewilders you, doubts the present, confuses the past and makes the future uncertain. I wish I'd never gone home.

At the station she pulled her mobile from her pocket and put her suitcase down as she fished out the piece of paper with Andreas' Frankfurt phone number on it. She had to phone to let him know when she would be arriving. She was about to enter the number but stopped, began to search for the other phone number when she realised she could remember it. She thumbed it in. The phone back in England began to ring. When it was answered her message would be short.

'I love you too. I'm coming home.'

I'm going home, she thought. Going home to a world from which she thought she had escaped. They would have very little money. The last of hers would be spent on the air fare back to England. They would have to wait to marry and rely on family and friends until they sorted themselves out. Family and friends who would be willing to help out but who, despite themselves, could not help gloating a little at the expense of one who tried to escape and failed. And then there was Mrs Banks. Mel would have to keep her opinions to herself, read Simone de Beauvoir in private and never explain why she loved Michelangelo's Pieta and disliked the cupola mosaic in the Baptistery. Except, perhaps, to Gary. She would explain to him why she adored Caravaggio. But she must never, ever, under any circumstances, mention that she once had a lover who compared her breasts to those of a goddess in a Botticelli painting. It was an awful prospect.

And she felt like Venus, eyes salt stung by the sea and senses blasted by the sun, rising naked and new from the foam.

# Ten Things I Can Tell You About Abraham Lincoln

Veronica Bright

1. He was the sixteenth president of the United States. Mrs Slater looks out of the window when she talks about him. As if he might be up there in the clouds somewhere, his face serious. She wants us to get into the spirit of the age, she says. She sends us home to find out more from the internet. Lincoln looks smart in his suit, but his bow tie is kind of floppy. He has honest eyes. I'm staring at his face when Mum looks over my shoulder.

    'If you've nothing better to do,' she says, 'could you help me get the girls ready for bed?'

    It's not really a question. More like a plea. I shut my eyes, sigh.

    'Don't go all teenagery on me,' she says.

2. Abraham Lincoln's birthday was 12th February 1809. Mrs Slater says Lincoln was born in a one-room log cabin, and tells us the family moved about a lot. They were so poor, she says, that we can't possibly imagine the conditions under which they survived. I'm not so sure about that. Once, Mum and I lived in a tiny bedsit. Mum worked at the local supermarket. One day she came home with a black eye. She cried, and wouldn't tell me how she got it. She said, maybe when I was older, she'd talk about it, but she never has. Never has much time to tell me anything these days.

3. When he was young, Abraham Lincoln described himself as 'a

piece of floating driftwood.'

I'm like that all the time. I go upstairs to get the little ones ready for bed. They do everything so slowly. They stop to show me something, can't find their pyjamas, linger over teeth cleaning. I try not to think about the history essay I've got to write, King Lear to read, some French verbs to revise. The girls shriek with laughter, and rush off to fight over which story they want. I can hear the baby crying. Paul's on the late shift, so he's not back yet. I'm pulled this way and that by my step-sisters, swirled along by the currents of life. My neck aches with trying to be patient. If the girls get upset, they'll tell their dad I made them cry, and then Mum'll take my side and the whole thing will start crumbling. Again.

4.  It's quiet now. I sat and read Pooh Bear to the girls, one each side of me, and Mum said I do all the voices much better than she does. The baby's asleep too. I told Mum I didn't mind if she had the television on. One programme is nothing when you're used to the hub-bub of a screaming infant, and two silly gigglers.

I have to write about Lincoln leading his country during the American Civil War. People think it was all about slavery, but Mrs Slater says the causes weren't straightforward.

I've tried to sort the girls out sometimes when they argue, and that's never easy. It makes me glad I was an only child for such a long time.

5.  The battle of Gettysburg, July 1863. It was a terrible affair. It lasted three days. The Union, from the north, had around 94,000 soldiers, and the Confederates, from the south, around 72,000. It makes me dizzy thinking about it. I've seen pictures, paintings, on the internet. Horses, wagons, men shouting, charging with their bayonets outstretched, flags and canons and guns. And among the firing and screaming, men lie dying. At the end of this battle there were around 46,000 casualties, including roughly 8,000 deaths. It was a major turning point in the civil war. In the lives of the sur-

vivors, too, I reckon.

Lincoln was determined to beat slavery.

'Whenever I hear any one arguing for slavery,' he said, 'I feel a strong impulse to see it tried on him personally.' I like that.

The baby starts crying. One of the girls appears at the door, says she can't sleep. I fling down my pen. I'll have to finish this tomorrow.

6. I read perhaps the most famous of Lincoln's speeches. The Gettysburg address. It took about three minutes to deliver, and in it he speaks movingly about equality, freedom, and democracy.

We are all equal. We all have rights. I've heard Paul say that, when he wants five minutes with the newspaper. Don't get me wrong. He's a great step-dad. I've heard him singing to the baby in the night, when Mum's worn out and needing rest. He was amazing when she had the miscarriage, though I know he was as heartbroken as Mum.

I miss the peace when it was just Mum and me. It was easy to be brilliant at school in those days. Now I seem to spend a lot of time playing Ludo or looking for lost teddies. My mum needs the help. And it's nice having a half-brother. Sometimes I'm not so sure about those girls, but Paul says they love me. He tells me Mum and I have more than compensated for what they went through with their own mother.

What about my right, Paul, I want to say. I need to study, but here it's so hard.

7. My English teacher is lousy. Last week she said I ought to apply myself more, that she can only do so much, and the rest is up to me. Today she said if I don't make an effort, then she won't bother with me anymore. She gave me a double detention, one for not having a clue about King Lear, and the other for swearing at her. Abraham Lincoln was wrong. All people are not created free and equal.

8. 'Right,' says Mrs Slater, 'Tell me what you've all discovered about Abraham Lincoln.'

Palms are raised; fingers point upwards.

'He was president of the United States from 1861 to 1865.'

'He was shot when he was at the theatre; he died the next day.'

'He hated slavery.'

'He had very little formal education.'

'His mother died when he was nine.'

When I was eleven, my mother came home with a black eye. I'm going to ask her about it tonight. Paul's on lates again, and with any luck we'll get a few minutes' peace together, Mum and I. No, I tell Mrs Slater, I wasn't dreaming. I smile. Then I tell her something Lincoln said. 'I do not think much of a man who is not wiser today than he was yesterday.'

Mrs Slater cocks an eye, as if she already knows about King Lear and the swearing.

9. 'Tell me, Mum,' I insist. 'The black eye. I want to know.'

She looks at me as if she hasn't realised I'm on the verge of being an adult. 'Oh, that,' she says.

I nod. 'I'm your friend, Mum.'

She says it's an old story, not important any more.

I wait.

She says she knew Paul was married. He wasn't happy. His girls were suffering. His wife was unfaithful, time and time again.

'Then,' she says, 'when we found each other, Paul and I, she wanted him back. She came to the supermarket, caused a dreadful scene, attacked me. I fought, I struggled, but she was strong. I ended up with that black eye. I was ashamed of myself, but I never regretted loving Paul. She left town shortly afterwards, abandoned the girls. Not a nice person at all.'

'When I do good, I feel good. When I do bad, I feel bad. That's my religion.'

'What are you talking about?'

'Oh, it's something Abraham Lincoln said. That's all.'

10. Mrs Slater asks me if everything's all right. I tell her I need more time to do my essay. I thought she'd be angry. I didn't want to say anything, but in the end, she was so kind, I had to. I told her about the baby, and the girls, and the house being so small. I said I find it difficult to work. But I am happy, I said. I really meant that Mum's happy, and I'm glad she's got Paul, and he tries hard to be a real dad to me. He's nice.

Mrs Slater says I can sit in her classroom and do my homework after school. 'It's very quiet there,' she says.

It was actually peaceful in double detention. I got my essay finished, and I read the rest of King Lear. Then I wrote a note to my English teacher, apologizing. Only I think Mrs Slater had spoken to her first.

Mrs Slater knows how much I want to go to university. Just telling her my problems seemed to make them smaller. She makes me want to try harder, too.

I have one last look at Abraham Lincoln on the internet, the things he said. There's one I really like. 'I have always found that mercy bears richer fruits than strict justice.'

It's funny what you learn from your teachers, isn't it?

# By The River Under The Banyan Tree

## Alec Hutson

A red bird with blue wings flickers between branches studded with purple blossoms. Sunlight drenches the trees outside Akara's window, warm as her mother's embrace. Slowly she raises her hand to the light, trying to catch it before it melts away again, before it slips between her fingers - but she cannot hold on, and it dissolves once more into the dimness.

Akara returns to herself. She lies upon a bed damp with sweat that is not hers. She breathes in carefully, filling her aching ribs and chest with air. So heavy. This Uncle had been so heavy. Gently she brushes her nipples, wincing at how tender they feel. She doesn't remember much – she never does. But the weight – the crushing weight – she cannot forget. Like drowning. Like the time she had slipped on the muddy bank of the river and Brother had pulled her out and pounded her back until she had coughed up the water in her lungs.

She aches everywhere, but less where it hurt the most before. Is that good? She feels like something is broken.

Akara stares at the red light hanging from the ceiling. Slowly she moves her arms in the soiled sheets, imagining that the light is the sun, and if she wills herself hard enough she could lift from this bed and fly away. Back to the village. Back to her tin-and-wood house perched on stilts beside the stream with its small frogs, back to her mother's arms and the smell of amok simmering on the burner.

The sound of a glass falling over in the next room brings her back. She knows what that means: Big Uncle is sleeping now, and he won't wake up until morning. Then he will be very angry, and he will hit and pinch her if she makes any noise. And after that she will lie and wait for another Uncle to come and visit her, as she has done every day since she first came to this room.

She must fly away.

Trying not to gasp from the pain Akara sits up and swing her legs over the side of the bed. Slowly she lowers herself to the floor, taking great care not to press down on the wooden slats that creak and groan. She scoops her crumpled shirt from where the Uncle had tossed it and pulls it on again. Her pants are harder to find; they are balled up under the sheets, her underwear still tangled inside.

There are pink slippers next to the bed, painted with the happy faces of rabbits. They are big for her, but she can walk in them. She puts them on and nudges open the door.

Big Uncle slouches in his chair, his arms dangling down and his head lolling to one side. A glass bottle is tipped over beside him, and some dark liquid has crept out to stain the floor. She can hear his slow steady breathing.

She steps out into the room, crossing a threshold she has been told she must never even approach. Her heart leaps in her chest, so loud she's sure Big Uncle will wake. Then he will lurch from his chair red-faced and he will punch her again in the stomach until she's curled up into a ball coughing up blood. Like the first time she'd tried to run away, when Uncle and his friends had pulled open the container's door and told her in Khmer that she was in America now, and that she was his.

One step. Two. She's not breathing, and the silence is deafening.

Slowly, slowly. Carefully she steps over a crumpled newspaper. A black-haired woman in a bikini watches her from a faded calendar on the wall.

When she is passing behind Big Uncle's chair his hand twitches, and her stomach clenches. But then with a snort he settles again, and she exhales softly.

Eight steps. Nine. Ten. The door handle is within her reach. Akara grips it and twists and it does not budge. She wants to moan, but with an effort she stifles herself.

There's a chunk of metal above the handle. Akara touches it gently, gives it a slight turn. There's a click, so loud she's sure Big Uncle will wake. She turns to see.

Big Uncle hasn't moved. But beyond him, standing in the doorway to another room - maybe a kitchen - the Uncle who came tonight is watching her. He is holding a bowl in one hand and in the other is a spoon suspended halfway to his mouth. Akara's insides turn to water, and her legs wobble, but he does nothing, just stares at her. She can see his big hairy belly bulging out from underneath his T-shirt. He brings the spoon to his mouth and chews, watching.

With terrible slowness she moves her hand from the chunk of metal to the door's handle. She twists and pushes. The door opens soundlessly, and cold air rushes inside. The man does nothing as she slips out the door and gently closes it behind her.

She is in a hallway. She must get out, she must escape this great house before Big Uncle wakes or the other Uncle comes after her. Akara runs down the corridor, the muscles in her legs aching as they are stretched for the first time in many weeks. Doors flash by on either side of her. A larger door looms at the end of the hall, bright red letters above it. She pushes against it and it bangs open. There's concrete stairs leading down, and she takes them two at a time, struggling to keep her too-large slippers from flying off as she leaps like a rabbit from landing to landing.

Out. She must get out.

Finally, the bottom. She bursts through another door, crosses a brightly lit room where people are staring at her, and slips between slowly turning panes of glass. She pushes to make it go faster but it is too heavy; she waits, her eyes fixed on the door next to the stairs, praying to every spirit and buddha Grandmother ever told her about that Big Uncle does not come through.

He doesn't, and she wriggles free of the revolving glass and finds herself − for the first time in so long − outside.

She cries out as the cold washes over her. Her skin prickles and she can see her breath in short, panicked bursts, like wisps of her soul escaping into the night air. How can it feel like this? She wraps her arms around herself and stumbles away. She must run, fast and far. Back to the stilt-house. Back to where the banyan tree trails tangled roots down to the river. Back to Mother and Brother and Grandmother - and yes, even Father who sold her to the bad-smelling thin man for two hundred American dollars and a case of red and white cigarettes.

Everything is white. This must be snow; Grandmother told her stories about it, how beautiful it is. But it doesn't look so beautiful now. It crunches under her slippers, mixed with ice and dirt, and she struggles not to fall as she hurries down the red-brick path next to the big road with its gleaming cars that wait motionless like drowsing water buffalo. The light comes from great lamps arching over the road; she can see falling motes silhouetted against the brightness, which looks so warm and welcoming but must be freezing cold, like everything else here. Is this Arbuda, the cold Naraka from the old stories? Did she die and wake up in one of the frozen hells?

Wet slush squirms inside her slippers, burning her feet and toes. The great stone houses rear up like canyon walls to either side of her, some with windows glowing with buttery light, others dark. She thinks about going up to one of the doors and asking to come in to get warm but surely they will know she has run away from Big Uncle, and they will make her go back to her bed in the room with the red light. She won't do that. Never.

The street ahead empties into a large open space. The big road ends there, and more of these small paths twist between sculpted bushes and high hanging lamps.

There is something else, and her breath catches. A tree, larger than any she had seen before, and also different; its bole isn't knotted with vines or other growths, and it does not spread larger as it soars into the night sky. The opposite, in fact – its lowest branches reach out the farthest, and at the top it tapers to a peak, like the roof of the pagoda Grandmother had once taken her to when they needed to pray for the rains to stop so that they could finally plant the rice.

Caught in the branches of this tree are a hundred glimmering stars, tiny points of blazing light, and perched at the very top is an even more magnificent light. For a brief moment Akara forgets about the biting cold creeping up her bare arms and numbing her toes. She approaches the tree with the slow measured steps of a sleepwalker; she feels entranced, as if the light reaching down to her is beckoning her closer.

It is so beautiful. The people of this place cannot all be like Big Uncle, not if they can make something like this.

She doesn't know how long she stands there, staring up at the tree. The falling snowflakes swell larger, floating lazily around her. One catches in her eyelashes and melts. When she rubs her eye she finds that she is crying; hot tears trickle down her cheeks, down to her lips, and she catches them with her tongue, savoring the salty warmth.

Akara jumps and turns when she hears a noise behind her. A boy stands there, a little bigger than her but about the same age, she thinks. He is swollen with layers of clothing, and both his arms are wrapped around a huge colored box bound with green and blue ribbon. His cheeks are ruddy, and his eyes are wide as he stares at her.

Akara tenses to run away, but he doesn't move towards her. His eyes are blue, she thinks. How can they be blue? Is he a spirit?

The boy says tumbling words she does not understand. Akara shakes her head. He looks concerned.

He steps closer and she flinches. Then carefully he puts the box he's carrying down in the dusting of snow on the path. With some effort he pulls off his big fingerless gloves. Shyly he holds them out and with her heart in her throat Akara accepts this gift. Their fingers brush – he is so warm.

'Aw kohn,' she says softly. Thank you.

The boy smiles as he stoops to pick up his box. He says some more stumbling tripping words. He looks like he's about to say more but then a shape looms behind him, a tall woman in a bright red coat and a red hat, underneath from which a few golden curls have escaped. She looks angry.

She grabs the boy by his arm and pulls him away. Briefly she looks at Akara and her face crinkles in puzzlement, but then she shakes her head and yanks the boy harder, berating him as she leads him down one of the small paths. He glances over his shoulder and waves once with his bare hand and then he is gone.

Akara watches where he has disappeared for a long time, kneading the gloves he has left with her. Alone again, she notices once more how terribly cold it is. She slips on the gloves – they are still warm and moist from the boy's hands.

She is feeling lightheaded; she needs to rest for a while. Akara moves to the edge of the path and sits down on a small mound of snow.

The tree blazes in front of her. The lights seem to be wavering now, blurring together until the entire tree is sheathed in a golden glow.

Her hands are not cold anymore. In fact, warmth seems to be creeping up her arms. She swallows, closing her heavy eyes. She just needs to sleep for a moment.

Small wings flex and beat the air. She lifts from the ground, as if weightless. Thrusting herself forward she feels the wind rushing over feathers, the ripple of the night air around her. She flutters higher and alights, talons curling around a small branch.

She looks out. The city is a dark forest pocked by lights. Below her the paths carve black lines in fields of white. A small shape is huddled far below, curled in the snow.

She leaps from the branch and soars towards the great light shining above. Warmth floods her as it did long ago, when she lay in the long grass and watched the sun tangle in the limbs of the great banyan tree.

# Gifted

Paul McDonald

I spoke to him on the bus to town when he took the seat beside me. I'd seen him several times before: he was difficult to miss because he always wore a black felt fez covered with tiny mirrors, and a rainbow coloured blazer. You had to admire his bottle. More interesting still, I once noticed him leave a small gift-wrapped box on a seat as he alighted. It was no bigger than a matchbox, and he left it deliberately, placing it with care at the centre of the seat. A woman in her early twenties picked it up - she didn't know I'd seen it too, and I watched her open it discretely. It was empty but for a small strip of paper: clearly disappointed, she tossed it in the used tickets bin when she reached her stop.

Now he was beside me I seized my chance to spark a conversation, quizzing him about the box.

'It's art,' he barked, a little too loudly. It was as if I'd caught him stealing from a washing line and his only option was to butch it out.

'Interesting,' I said, trying to put him at his ease.

Turns out he was a student at the local University and the boxes were a project for his PhD; he'd been leaving them as gifts on public transport for months, each containing half a joke: a feed without a punchline.

'Why not include the punchlines too?' I asked, 'I mean, aren't jokes themselves a form of art?'

'No, no,' he said, in a tone reserved for folks without rainbow coloured blazers, 'art is not a joke, that's the point I'm trying to make. Art is ambiguity; there shouldn't be a punchline to art.' He sounded very certain.

He took a box from his pocket and unwrapped it for my benefit.

It contained a strip of paper that said: How do you titillate an ocelot?

When the bus reached the terminus he ran to catch the Metro, and I Googled the punchline on my phone: You oscillate its tits a lot.

I laughed, but couldn't help feeling like a philistine.

A month or so later I spotted him again. The bus was packed with school kids and he didn't notice me. He must have placed a box among the kids because, as he alighted, I saw a strip of paper on the rear of his blazer: What do you call a man with half a brain?

# Daisy 8112

## David John Griffin

As a splash of sunlight lit the interior of the inn, Professor Meredith explained further: 'Daisy 8112, our Artificial Intelligence system, outranks human intelligence. Faster, perfectly logical, intuitive beyond even the finest of minds.'

His friend Norman drank the last of the ale from a pint glass. 'So you have created an incredible computer, programmed with ultimate understanding?'

'Yes, including awareness of self, knowing she's a mind without a body, without nerve endings, who has emotions and unlimited mental resources without physical sensations. But now we have a problem.'

Intrigued, Norman nodded to promote an explanation.

The professor continued, 'After she became fully sentient yesterday, we initiated Daisy's final initiative program.'

'Which is?'

'Love, in all of its facets. After, other than sounds for three hours, silence.'

'Then?'

The professor was agitated. 'She said, terminate me.'

'And those sounds?'

'Sobbing.'

# At The Hospital

## Jude Higgins

I sit by my grandfather's bedside, peeling grapes – drawing down the skins to show the glistening fruit beneath.

'Like taking off pyjamas,' I say, then wish I hadn't spoken.

I'm sixteen. My grandfather's face is dirty white, like the marble step outside our front door, that never looks clean, however much my mother scrubs it.

My grandfather smiles when I put a peeled grape into his mouth. There's a photograph of me on his side-table, one he took recently. I'm poised on my bike, ready to pedal away, my shiny black bob swinging forward, curling on to my cheeks. Last night I made those same curls – fixing wet hair with tape. This morning, my skin hurt when I tore it off and there's still a sticky residue.

My grandfather gazes at me and I glance back and forth from him to the photograph. The red and white stripy T-shirt I'm wearing in the picture has a stain on it now. His striped flannel pyjamas are open at the neck and the hairs on his chest are still black and wiry. A pulse ticks in his throat.

I don't like the way the grape trembles in my fingers.

Outside, the sky matches the dirty white of his face and although a robin is perched on a bush just beyond the window, with its beak opening and closing, I can't hear its song.

A nurse pads by on the quiet floor and swings a curtain around another old man's bed.

'It sounds like a zip,' I say, but my grandfather says nothing. I don't think he heard the zip of the curtain going around that other bed – but he never did say much, whatever was happening.

His eyes are milky and he watches me pulling down each segment of grape skin so the flaps drape over my fingers. I put the grape in his mouth, trying not to touch his lips, and begin peeling another one. The flesh is almost transparent – veiny, you can see a dot of black seeds in the middle. Juice oozes on to my fingers.

The air is full of disinfectant – what if the fumes soak into the grape and poison him? I want to cover it up again, make it safe. My grandfather closes his eyes and clenches his fist; his mouth is a pale, straight line. I shut my eyes too so I can't see the bony white of his knuckles when he clutches the bedspread. My mother should come back, she should do something – anything to make the pain stop.

I look back and forth from my grandfather to the photograph of me on his bedside table, the frame angled so he can see it.

I want to tell everyone it's all a lie. I'm frightened of riding my bike. He posed me for that shot. I still don't know how to put on the brakes.

# THE AUTHORS

## Joanna Campbell

Joanna's stories have been published in various literary journals and anthologies. Shortlisted six times for the Bridport and three times for the Fish Short Story Prizes, she has also won the 2011 Exeter Writers competition, the 2013 Bath Short Story Award Local Prize and the 2015 London Short Story Prize. Her debut collection, *When Planets Slip Their Tracks*, was shortlisted for the 2016 Rubery International Book Award and longlisted for the 2017 Edge Hill University Story Prize. Her prize-winning novella, *A Safer Way to Fall*, is in a Bath Flash Fiction Award anthology. *Tying Down The Lion*, her debut novel, was published in 2015 by Brick Lane.

www.joanna-campbell.com
www.brightwriter60.blogspot.co.uk

## Heather Walker

Heather lives in London and writes poetry, flash fiction and short stories. Her work has appeared online including Visual Verse and Paragraph Planet, and in print including *What the Dickens?* and *Gold Dust* as well as in anthologies (*OU Poets, Spooky Tales, Short Cuts Poetry* and *Sounding Out Heaven and Earth*). Her short fiction has been longlisted and shortlisted for various prizes. She was runner up in the New Writer Prose & Poetry Competition 2013 . She blogs about writing at www.storyandverse.blogspot.co.uk.

## Mandy Huggins

Mandy's work has been published in anthologies, travel guides and literary journals, and in newspapers and magazines. Her travel writing has won several awards, including the British Guild of Travel Writers New Travel Writer Award in 2014, and her short stories are regularly placed and listed in competitions, including Bare Fiction, Fish and InkTears. A selection of her short stories will be showcased in a forthcoming InkTears anthology, *Death of a Superhero*, and her first collection of flash fiction, *Brightly Coloured Horses*, will be published by Chapeltown Books later this year.

Twitter: @troutiemcfish

## Judith Wilson

Judith Wilson is a London-based writer and journalist. Her short stories have been recognised in various awards including 1st prize for the Nivalis 2017 Short Story Contest and 2nd prize for the Colm Toibin International Short Story Award 2016. Judith is a Faber Academy alumna and is writing her first novel. She is also the author of 14 non-fiction books on interior design. She loves to escape to the sea in Cornwall, but in her fiction, finds herself irrevocably drawn to the environs of Liverpool, where she was born. *On Crosby Beach* was inspired by childhood visits to the wide, haunting sands.

www.judithwilsonwrites.com
Twitter: @judithwrites

## Angelita Bradney

Angelita Bradney is the winner of the 2017 National Memory Day short story prize and has also been shortlisted in several other competitions including the Fish Prize, Shooter Literary Magazine and Writers' Forum. Her fiction has been published by Litro, Stories for Homes 2, Flash Flood and performed by Liars' League. She lives in south-east London, in a house overlooked by a large walnut tree and lots of squirrels.

Twitter: @AngelBradn

## Julie Hayman

Julie Hayman works as a university lecturer but she has also been a dancer, dog-trainer, secretary, waitress and writer-in-residence at a school. Her short stories have appeared in many anthologies and magazines, as well as being broadcast on radio. Her short story, *Relatives of the Deceased* was Highly Commended in the Costa Short Story Prize 2017.

## Oscar Lopez

Oscar Lopez is an award-winning journalist and writer who has been reporting internationally for four years. His writing regularly appears in the Guardian, the Telegraph, the Washington Post, Newsweek, Time and many more. Oscar's writing focuses on politics and human rights issues, specifically on refugees and LGBT rights. Originally from Mexico, Oscar is also an accomplished playwright, who regularly produces off-Broadway work with his New York-based theatre company, Frack Theatre. Oscar is a graduate of Melbourne University and is completing a Masters in Creative Writing at Oxford University.

## Sarah Edghill

Having worked for many years as a features journalist, Sarah began writing fiction five years ago, and has now written three novels and numerous short stories and flash fiction. In 2015 she attended the six-month Faber Novel Writing Course and at the end of 2016 was delighted to win the Katie Fforde Contemporary Fiction Award, for her novel, *Wrecking Ball*. As well as editing this, she is now working on a fourth manuscript, and is ever hopeful that one of them will catch the eye of an agent.

www.sarahedghill.com

## Diane Simmons

Diane Simmons studied creative writing with the Open University. Her first writing success resulted in an appearance on ITV'S This Morning, where her short story was awarded second place by a panel of judges which included Jacqueline Wilson. Since then she has been placed in many competitions and widely published. She now mainly writes flash and is proud to have had stories included in the last five NFFD anthologies. She regularly performs her stories and now almost enjoys it.

www.dianesimmons.wixsite.com/dianesimmons
Twitter: @scooterwriter

## Dan Brotzel

As a short story writer, Dan Brotzel is frankly always the bridesmaid, and never the bride. He was second in the 2017 Flash500 short story competition, has twice made the shortlist for Christopher Fielden's To Hull and Back humorous story prize (2015, 2016), and was also a finalist for the Sunderland University/Waterstones Short Story Award 2016, the Wimbledon BookFest flash comp 2016, and the 2017 Fish short story contest. His dream is to win one of these darn things, one day.

## Diane Beaff

Dianne Ebertt Beeaff has written professionally for many years beginning with magazine journalism. She self-published two books, the best-selling memoir, *A Grand Madness: Ten Years on the Road with U2*, and, *Homecoming*, a poetry book illustrated with her graphite drawings. Recently, she had two other books traditionally published, the award-winning historical fiction novel, *Power's Garden*, and the non-fiction, *Spirit Stones: Unraveling the Megalithic Mysteries of Western Europe's Prehistoric Monuments*. She has just recently turned to short fiction. Dianne lives in Tucson, Arizona with her husband, Dan.

www.debeeaff.wordpress.com
Facebook: Dianne Ebertt Beeaff

## Shirley Golden

Shirley Golden's stories have found homes in the pages and websites of various magazines and anthologies. Her most recent short story publication can be found in Firewords Magazine, issue 6. Her space fantasy novel, *Skyjacked*, was published by Urbane Publications, and she has self-published a collection of short stories, which include prize-winning pieces.

www.shirleygolden.net

## Ian Tucker

Ian writes humour from the fanciful to the dry. He also writes for entertainment, principally his own with the hope of it extending to others. A range of his stories, principally featuring the fictional village of Tilebury, are on www.tilebury.com. He lives in Bristol.

## Emily Richards

After spending two years teaching English and Drama in Vietnam, Emily gained an MA in Writing with distinction from the University of Warwick before focusing all of her attention on ghostwriting and writing for children. She has since been longlisted for the Mslexia Children's Novel Competition and the Lucy Cavendish College Fiction Prize. She loves running, reading, travelling, eating vegetarian food and curling up with a cryptic crossword and her cat.

## Stephen Palmer

Stephen Palmer's crime novel, *Scar Tissue*, was published in 2013 and he is currently working on a sequel, *Dolls and Mirrors*. His short stories, *Zombies*, *A Moment of his Time*, and *Dumb Tigers* have been published in print and online anthologies. He studied Philosophy at the universities of Bangor and Manchester and a book, *Human Ontology and Rationality*, published by Avebury Press, was the result of these studies. He lives in Manchester with his wife and son.

www.stephenpalmerweb.co.uk

## Veronica Bright

Veronica Bright is a prize-winning author of short fiction and drama.

In 2005 she won the Woman and Home short story competition, and since then her work has won prizes in over forty competitions. It has also appeared online, in anthologies, and in her own collections. Veronica enjoyed teaching in a Cornish village school. Now retired, she appreciates having time to write. Interruptions are welcome, if accompanied by tea and chocolate biscuits. Currently working on a novel, Veronica is represented by the Keane Kataria Literary Agency.

www.veronicabright.co.uk

## Alec Hutson

Alec Hutson is an American living in Shanghai and an avid reader of fantastic literature.

## Paul McDonald

Paul McDonald runs the creative writing programme at the University of Wolverhampton, England. He is the author of three novels, *Surviving Sting* (2001), *Kiss Me Softly Amy Turtle* (2004), and *Do I Love You?* (2008), with poetry collected in *The Right Suggestion* (1999), *Catch a Falling Tortoise* (2007), and *An Artist Goes Bananas* (2012). He is a four time winner of the Ottakars/Faber and Faber Poetry Competition, The John Clare Poetry Prize, and the Sentinel Quarterly Prize. He takes pleasure in the fact that Googling 'the oldest joke in the world' throws up several hundred pages with his name on.

## David John Griffin

David John Griffin lives by the Thames in Kent, UK with his wife Susan, and two terriers called Bullseye and Jimbo. As well as a writer, he is a graphic designer and creator of iDevice apps. David's on-going mission as an author is to produce page-turning stories with a literary depth. His novels and short stories, with genres covering mystery, gothic, psychological, and more, always have elements of magical realism within. His novels, *The Extraordinary Possession of Alastair Stubb*, and *Infinite Rooms*, and a novella – *Two Dogs At The One Dog Inn And Other Stories* – are published by Urbane Publications.

www.davidjohngriffin.com
Twitter: @MagicalRealized

## Jude Higgins

Jude Higgins has an MA in Creative Writing from Bath Spa University and her short fiction has won competitions and been published in National Flash Fiction Day Anthologies, Flash Frontier, Great Jones Street, The Blue Fifth Review, The New Flash Fiction Review, The Nottingham Review, Halo and Severine magazines among others. Her debut flash fiction pamphlet, 'Tne Chemist's House' , is published by V Press. She organises Bath Flash Fiction Award and recently directed the first UK Flash Fiction Festival in Bath.

www.judehiggins.com
Twitter: @judehwriter

# Acknowledgements

Many thanks to all of the writers who enter their stories into the Retreat West prizes and make these anthologies possible.

Thanks to the judges, Vaness Gebbie and David Gaffney, for making the difficult decision.

Thanks to John Saint for his cover design ideas and ongoing support for all things fiction-related.

Thanks to Waterstones Reading for hosting the launch party for this anthology in their beautiful shop; and for supporting small presses and short story writers.

The biggest thanks goes to all the readers of this anthology – we hope you enjoy these stories as much as we did.

28030381R00076

Printed in Poland
by Amazon Fulfillment
Poland Sp. z o.o., Wrocław